Stories from
Outer Space

Stories from
Outer Space

Raj Sacranie
Illustrated by
John Gosler

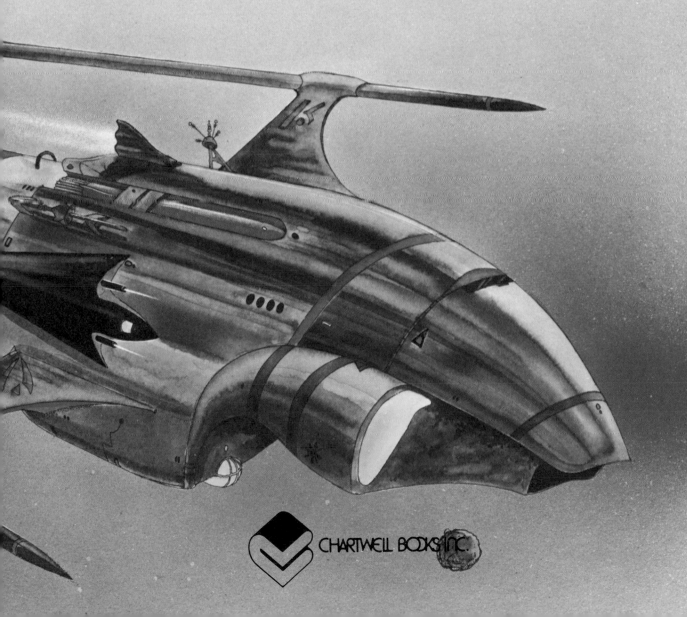

CHARTWELL BOOKS INC.

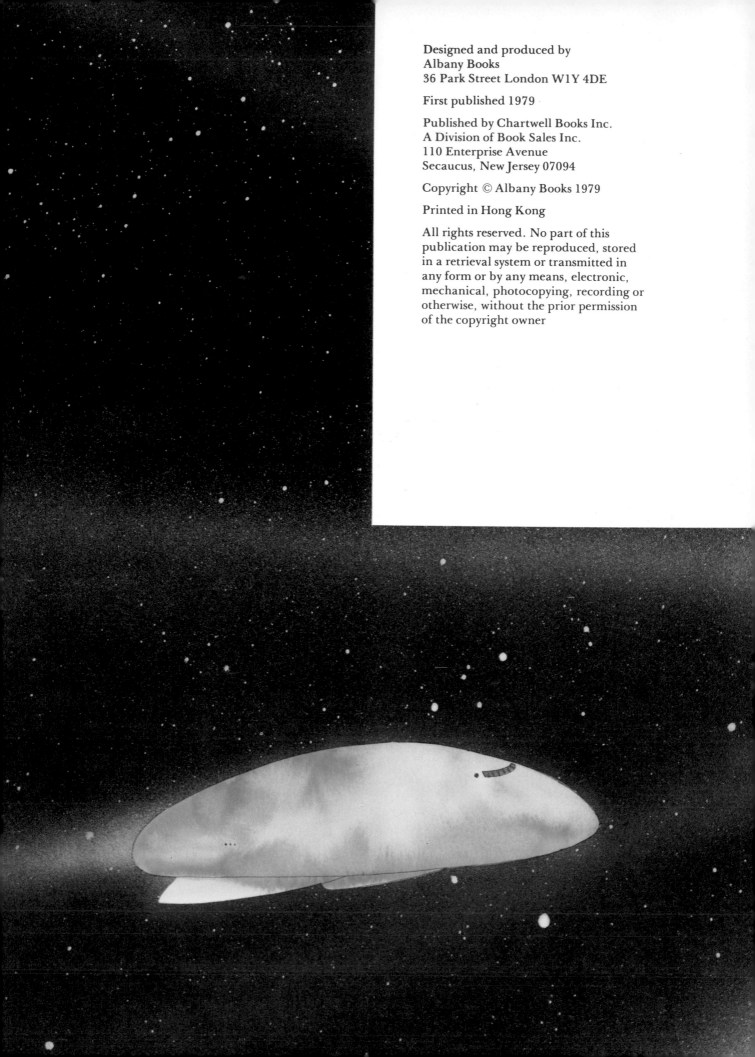

Designed and produced by
Albany Books
36 Park Street London W1Y 4DE

First published 1979

Published by Chartwell Books Inc.
A Division of Book Sales Inc.
110 Enterprise Avenue
Secaucus, New Jersey 07094

Copyright © Albany Books 1979

Printed in Hong Kong

Contents

Edgar

When a slightly timorous human being lands on an unfamiliar planet without a job or a place to live, what confidence he started with evaporates rapidly. And when that planet is the meeting-cum-market place of a thousand species his senses are bludgeoned by the sheer diversity of cultures to the point where he is unable to absorb any more and retreats into his merely human shell.

Carson was such a timid human: a small, mild man from Earth. He found himself in the city of Callo, on the planet of Riga, almost by accident. He was the only survivor of the spaceship *Antares,* which was bound for the human colony on Adler when it was hit amidships by a rogue comet. He was picked up by a Federation cruiser, clucked at sympathetically by the crew of Andromedans and told that it would not be possible either to take him on to Adler, where he had an accountant's job waiting for him, or back to Earth. The best they could do was to take him to Riga, where he might eventually find passage to Adler. So Carson acquiesced: he had no choice and anyway he found the Andromedans, with their fiery eyes and wicked talons, rather daunting.

Callo made Carson feel terribly insignificant. The city catered to the needs of every known sentient species; consequently there was a bewildering variety of sights, colours, sounds

and smells constantly hitting him in the face. He was intensely aware of the indifference all big cities demonstrate towards the stranger, and this one seemed more careless of his presence than most. Aliens brushed past and stepped over him as if he didn't exist; he was nearly run down by unconcerned maniacs in flitters and ground-cars more than once, and he couldn't find anyone to tell him how to locate a place to live or something to eat. Ten minutes of hovering indecisively at the entrance to the spaceport and he was sure that even the buildings around him were looking at him and laughing at his shortcomings. And the tension in him coiled up tighter and tighter, until it seemed as if the skin of his body was splitting at the seams and his human spirit was going to seep out to disappear into the sewers of this uncaring city.

Then he met Edgar. It was the first living creature in that city which seemed to answer the plea in his eyes. It looked at him cordially as he fought to keep his balance in the buffeting of the multicultured throng. It sandwiched itself between Carson and the wall and, once sheltered by the human's body, spoke to him in a strange language. Carson didn't understand a word, but got the impression that it was comforting him, telling him, "Yes, I know. Once I was confused too, but if the two of us stay together everything will be fine." The creature looked carefully at Carson and, reassured by the man's smile, took his hand and drew him through the crowds to a relatively deserted bar in a side-street a short distance from the spaceport. Carson resisted initially at the touch of the alien's furry paw, then shrugged his shoulders and allowed himself to be led.

In the bar the creature called out for service in Galactic, and Carson had the opportunity to look closely at it while it was ordering. It looked remarkably like a large cat with lilac fur and an attenuated tail. It had warm, amber eyes in a mobile, almost feminine face. Its paws, which it was waving around in exasperation at the robot waiter's non-comprehension, were like delicately furred human arms, ending in razor-sharp claws which it kept retracted except when it was annoyed. The lilac fur extended all over its body except for a burst of red at its chest and throat. The body itself was lean, almost

skeletal. Carson's examination was interrupted when the alien, having settled matters with the robot to its satisfaction, looked at him with warm eyes and smiled. Carson smiled back: it seemed as natural as the act of breathing.

"The waiters here are obsolete. They cannot understand the simplest instruction. I have ordered pique for you. As a human you will find it quite pleasant," it said in a purring voice. "My name is Xlp. You will have difficulty pronouncing that so you may call me Edgar. That is what my last human — companion called me."

Carson felt a wave of gratitude at the unassuming way this cat-like creature offered its friendship. He sat back in his seat and seemed to breathe easily for the first time since he had landed on Riga.

"Where are you from?" he asked Edgar.

"I'm from —" Edgar hesitated, "— a planet at the Outer Rim. It was destroyed five hundred years ago by the Denebians. Those of us who survived have scattered all over the galaxy. I suppose you could almost call Riga my home, if that is at all possible. Riga is a planet for transients. And you — you are from Earth?"

"Yes." Carson told the alien his story. "That's when you found me. I must confess that I was a little worried when I was waiting at the spaceport. I didn't know what to do. I have very little money and I have to find a job to pay for my passage on to Adler. I also have no place to live, and this city is so *strange* —" He broke off as the drinks ordered by Edgar materialized. A glass of a rosy liquid, smoking slightly over the sides, was placed in front of him. He sipped at it, intrigued by the sensation of smoke spilling down his throat. It was delicious, and he told Edgar so.

"Yes. Pique is a great favourite with humans. And they make it well here. It compensates for the terrible service. Now, let us consider your problems. We will find you a place to live without any difficulty. We will try to make your money last until you find a job. As for the strangeness of the city —" Edgar paused, and looked searchingly at Carson. "I know this city better than most species, and all the traps and snares it holds for the unwary. I have accompanied other humans before. I am willing to be your companion now, for as long as you need me." It held up a paw as Carson stirred uncertainly. "If you are worried about my fee, I assure you that it is minimal. All I ask is that you let me stay with you and that you feed me. And when you leave, as you are bound to do one day, that you answer one question. That is all. Is it not a reasonable bargain?"

Carson considered. He did not doubt Edgar's friendliness, but was wary of being taken

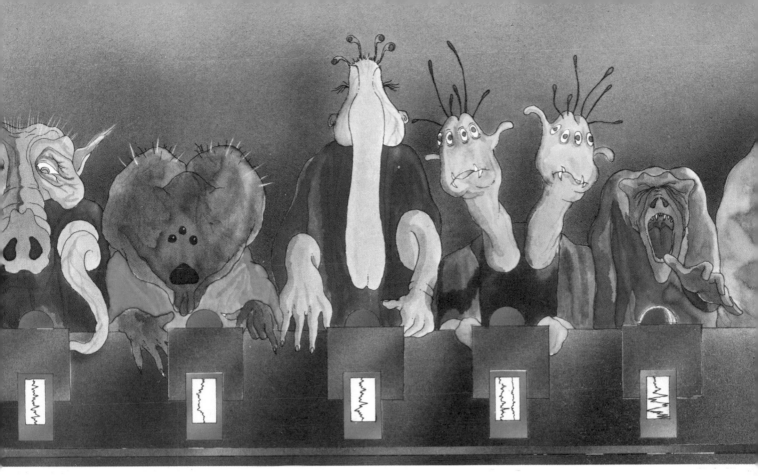

advantage of; and suppose Edgar had some nefarious purpose in mind, like robbing him or, even worse, doing him some sort of physical hurt? But one look at Edgar dissolved these latter fears. He didn't have enough money to be worth a thief's attention, and how could he suspect such a compassionate, warm creature of threatening him in any way? There was, however, the 'question'.

"What is this question you want to ask me when I leave? Why can't you ask it now?"

Edgar's reply was immediate. "Because you cannot hope to understand me sufficiently to be capable of answering it now. Is it a bargain?"

Carson didn't hesitate long before answering.

With Edgar's help Carson found a three-roomed flat, utilitarian but adequate, the same day. That evening he discovered that he was comfortable with the alien. It did not solicit conversation, but was content simply to be available and answer any questions Carson cared to ask. It seemed to have an almost uncanny appreciation of the nuances of the human's moods and could shift with them from sobriety to irreverent facetiousness with ease. Carson discovered that it knew of no other members of its own species on Riga, and had few friends in Callo. This was because Callo was a terminus: everyone left eventually. No, it was seldom lonely; it generally found companion-

ship of some sort, which had led to some awkward adventures — like the time when a Syllphian had decided that it, Edgar, must be good to eat, and had tried quite hard to prove the point; or another occasion when it had played nursemaid to a family of Nugs — all six thousand of them. What about the times when it was not escorting anyone? Those didn't occur too often, and it always seemed to survive. What happened to the other humans you acted as companion to? A shrug; they left Riga. Did they answer your question? Yes, but it was not the answer I wanted.

The next morning Carson found a job. There were very few humans in Callo, and consequently little call for his particular skills as an accountant. Nevertheless he was taken on as an overseer at a factory that produced souvenirs of Riga for tourists. He found himself in charge of an assembly line manned by aliens of every description — a riot of species and languages, with only two things in common: they all spoke Galactic after a fashion when pressed, and they were all destitute. The work they did was the most menial anywhere in the galaxy. All they were required to do was press a series of buttons in a selected sequence, at great speed; it was Carson's job to decide how quickly he could make them work. Every creature on the assembly line, including Carson himself, had a

device strapped to an arm or leg which administered a violent shock whenever a mistake was made or work was proceeding too slowly. Carson was not invulnerable to this sophisticated goad: if he slowed down the assembly line out of compassion for the workers' exhaustion, more often than not he was punished extremely painfully. So he dared not let up on his charges, and by the end of his first shift he was a mass of nerves.

When he got back that evening he discovered that as long as he was with Edgar he could drive the horror of his work to the back of his mind. It was almost as if Edgar's presence was a denial of horror and uncertainty. The creature moved slowly and with certain grace. It looked at everything with unblinking serenity. Edgar gave the impression that it did not believe in chance, that everything progressed in a logical, pre-destined order and that there was nothing to be apprehensive about. Carson discovered that when he was with the alien his mind smoothed out: the knots of anxiety and worry which were so much a part of his life loosened and his heart beat more quietly. And during the next few weeks Edgar introduced him painlessly to Callo.

They toured the city in a flitter. It stretched out for thousands of kilometres in every direction and stunned Carson with its complexity and infinite variety. He enthused about it: surely, somewhere in the city, there must be perfection for every being in Creation. Edgar replied sardonically that there was; and that it might take a being's lifetime to find that perfection.

They wallowed in the Catacombs of Callo — or rather, Carson did, and Edgar kept an eye on him. The Catacombs were the red-light district of the city and the sort of place where for a price you could experience ecstacies beyond your wildest imaginings, as they say. This was probably the most dangerous part of Callo and Carson was grateful more than once that Edgar was around to extricate him from his own follies.

They went to a mountain in the centre of Callo. There was a guard-rail round the mountain, and when Carson looked at it looming high above him he felt a vertigo that seemed to pull him over the rail, and a shattering intelligence probing at his brain; had it not been for Edgar's restraining paw and its firmness he would surely have been engulfed. A safe distance away from the mountain the alien

14

explained what Carson had seen and experienced: the mountain was pure intelligence, utterly incomprehensible to any contemporary species; it was constantly adding to its store of information and once it had established a hold over another creature it never relaxed it. Fortunately its reach was limited. It was the only native inhabitant of Riga, and the only one who could truly call Riga its home. Carson looked curiously at Edgar when it said this, sensing some underlying sadness; when the alien did not elaborate he asked why it had not been affected by the mountain. "It has no high opinion of my potential," replied Edgar, with some dryness.

They visited the museums which displayed the history and achievements of a thousand species. Carson wandered around the immense chambers and was filled with awe at the grandeur of the exhibits; he had never felt his own insignificance as sharply as he did now, when he was faced with the achievements and nobility of so many other species, whereas the entire history of the human race rated only one small chamber. It occurred to Carson that Edgar's species must be represented here, and he asked the alien if they could see it. For the

first time Edgar grew agitated. "Yes, there is an exhibit. But it is incomplete, and it is very important to me that you do not see it yet. It will prevent you from answering with any degree of accuracy the question I mean to ask you before you leave. I beg you not to press me to show it to you now." Carson instantly agreed, but a small seed of doubt was sown in his mind.

The days and weeks drifted by. Carson went to work each day and stumbled back to the accommodation he shared with Edgar each evening. He learned to harden himself to his unpleasant duties and was punished less often. Nevertheless, he developed an abiding hatred for his employers and, indirectly, for the culture which allowed the use of such goads to ensure optimum production. He developed a dependence on Edgar which transcended the bargain they had struck: he realized this only when he became aware that he had not seen another human being for many months, and not for one moment had he missed the companionship of his own species.

One evening they were sitting in a bar, drinking pique. They were discussing in a desultory fashion the advantages of going to see the spectacular four-dimensional multi-spatial opera which had just opened. The bar was very noisy: an entire platoon of the Space Corps had descended on it and were intent on drinking themselves into stupefaction in the shortest possible time. Polyglot conversations crackled through the air like fireworks; fights erupted spontaneously and ended abruptly; songs were sung lustily and tears were shed; and the bar rocked with merrymaking. Carson and Edgar gave up their discussion when it became clear that they were not going to be able to hear each other shout, and sat back to watch the soldiers get progressively drunker.

Then one soldier, a massive, vaguely humanoid creature, staggered to the table where the friends were sitting. He peered first at Carson, obviously thinking that the human was someone else, shook his head in disappointment when he failed to identify him, glanced at Edgar — and froze, staring as if he could not believe his eyes. Carson was astonished to see Edgar jump to its feet and make for the door of the bar; and his astonishment turned to fear for his friend when the soldier, moving very quickly for all his bulk, cut Edgar's retreat off and with

a single haymaking swipe sent the alien crashing against the wall.

Carson was not a brave man, but before he had time to think he found himself on his feet, wrestling with Edgar's antagonist. The soldier turned on him and, lifting him with contemptuous ease into the air, flung him across the room to land with a thump on a table, scattering drinks and sunflowers who were sipping placidly. Carson went berserk at this treatment. He had never been involved in a fight before and the blood-lust that roared in his veins was a new and pleasurable sensation . . . and Edgar was still lying on the floor by the wall, apparently unconscious. Carson catapulted himself off the table and flew at the soldier, picking up a broken bottle as he made his rush. The soldier hesitated when he saw this little figure bearing down on him, and his hesitation undid him. Carson slammed into him. The burly figure crumpled to the floor and Carson was on him, bottle poised to gouge at the eyes.

He was pulled off the soldier before he could do any more damage. It took him a long time to

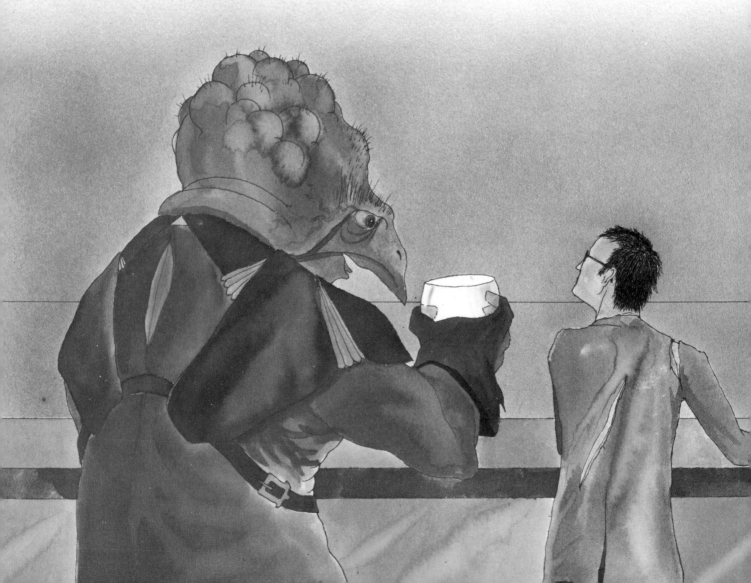

recover from the insanity that had gripped him. When he had regained control of himself and was released he went across to the stirring Edgar to make sure that the alien was all right. To his complete surprise when Edgar saw him coming it struggled to its feet and, with one incredibly pleading look at the human, disappeared through the door of the bar. Carson ran to the entrance and peered out through the night: there was no sign of his friend. He called out a few times, with no response. Rather reluctantly he returned to the bar.

The racket, which had ebbed while the fight was taking place, was going full blast again. Carson was a little apprehensive to see the massive soldier come purposefully towards him. His rage had dissipated entirely and he could not see himself continuing the fight, but the soldier was smiling broadly; before Carson had time to take any avoiding action he was enveloped in a vast bearhug.

"You're a good scrapper for a little man. Let me buy you a drink," the soldier said in Galactic, steering Carson to the bar. The human was too overpowered to refuse. "But you must be more careful who you drink with." The soldier squinted at him. "Especially scum like that coward who ran away."

"What do you mean? What are you talking about?"

"Don't you know who that was?"

"Of course I do. That was Edgar — its real name is Xlp — it's a friend of mine."

"You can't be serious. Don't you realize *what* it is?"

"I don't know what you're talking about."

The soldier examined Carson with some distaste. "That creature was a Bran."

"So what? What's a Bran?"

"You don't know what a Bran — ah, you must be from Earth. They don't know anything in that backwater. Well, I'll tell you, and you can be sure that you'll no longer call it your friend." He took a vast gulp of his drink and began.

"The Bran lived on a planet called Prima on the Outer Rim. They were — are — extremely long-lived and by the time first contact was made they had developed to the point where they had virtually eliminated illness. But space flight was unknown to them and they were confined to just one planet. As a result the only way they could control their own population was by waging incessant war, and they developed extremely sophisticated weaponry. The arrival of the Federation survey ship was their salvation. And the Emperor at the time was Cal X — you must have heard of him, even on Earth — who saw how they could be used. They enjoyed fighting and were the best soldiers in the galaxy — so he built them up into the most powerful fighting force in recorded history. With their help Cal X soon controlled most of the galaxy.

Then the Emperor was assassinated — and the Bran decided to continue where he had left off. They broke up into smaller groups and seized as much territory as they could for themselves. For the next two hundred years the entire galaxy was terrorized by them. Populations were wiped out, planetary systems were destroyed, and, when nearly the whole galaxy was under the control of this vile species, the Bran turned their talents to fighting each other. This was the Interregnum, when many species, including mine, were forced into slavery to produce the weapons the Bran needed. Then, when it seemed as if they were going to blow the Universe apart, they developed a biological weapon — an extremely contagious virus — against which they themselves had no defence. They died like flies when it got out of control. Other species were immune. Eventually the galaxy was free of them; the only pocket left was a small population on Prima, their home world. The disease passed, and the reconstituted Federation decided that there were too few Bran left to worry about."

The soldier sighed and ordered more drinks. Carson was lost in the story and drank down his second pique without noticing it. When the soldier looked pointedly at him he remembered his responsibilities and ordered another round. Then the soldier continued.

"The Federation was wrong. It took the Bran only one hundred years to burst out of Prima and engulf the galaxy in fighting again. But this time the Federation was united against them from the beginning, and had superior numbers; still the war was savage and lasted twenty years. When the Bran were beaten very little was left of the thirty planetary systems closest to Prima. One of them was the home of my species. We have been forced to be nomads ever since, those of us who survived. This time the Federation made no mistake. Prima was obliterated. The only Bran left alive were those in prison camps and laboratories all over the galaxy; not more than a few thousand. The Federation tolerates them now, but makes sure that they remain scattered on places like Riga, where they can keep an eye on them."

The soldier sighed heavily. Then his voice took on an implacable note. "That's why I

attacked the vermin you were with. My species has a very long memory. If I ever see it again I will destroy it."

When Carson finally left the bar he was very drunk. He reeled back to the flat, expecting to find Edgar there. He was angry at the alien's deception and horrified by the story, but at the same time he was haunted by its kindnesses and easy companionship. Edgar wasn't there, however, and failed to make an appearance on succeeding days.

Carson continued to go to work and to wander alone around the city in his spare time. He spent a lot of time going from bar to bar and revisited all the tourist spots, hoping to find the little alien, with no success. He was desperately lonely, and his timidity in the face of the anonymity of this city returned.

He also went back to the museum, where he located the exhibit for Prima and the Bran. What he learned was essentially the same as the soldier had told him, but he got a very much clearer idea of the tragedy of the Bran; and found it in his heart to feel a curious pity for the few survivors and the way they were separated from each other.

One year after he had arrived Carson had saved enough money to take passage back to Adler. He gave up his job with relief and waited for the spaceship, which would be arriving in three days. It was three months since he had last seen Edgar, and he had missed the alien.

The day before he was due to take ship the doorchime sounded. That surprised Carson for a moment: no-one ever visited him — and then he realized it could only be Edgar.

He let the alien into the flat. Edgar looked at him with its warm eyes and smiled, raising a paw in greeting. Carson smiled back, feeling ridiculously pleased. Then he remembered what the creature was and his smile grew stiff. Edgar, as always, was sensitive to his moods, and looked at him gravely.

"So you know all about me now?"

"Yes."

"But are you sure you know the whole story?"

"What more is there to tell?"

"So, my friend, you feel you can make an accurate judgement? As all my other companions did?"

Carson didn't answer for a few minutes. Then the weight of the galaxy's judgement on Edgar's species prevailed, and he mumbled, "Yes, I think I can."

Edgar's shoulders seemed to slump slightly as it read Carson's face. "But it's been five hundred years. Can you not allow for the possibility that my species has changed since then?"

Carson thought about it, his every instinct screaming out for him to say Yes. Edgar had proved to him without a shadow of a doubt that the character of the Bran *had* changed. His struggle was reflected in the sweat pouring from his face.

Edgar sighed and shrugged its elegant shoulders. Then it went to the door and opened it. It turned around to face Carson.

"I can't argue with your decision. After all, the galaxy agrees with you. I wish you a safe and pleasant journey to Adler."

Edgar turned and started out of the door. Carson was paralyzed for a moment, then shouted, "Wait!" The alien stopped and looked inquiringly at him. "What was the question you wanted to ask me?"

When Edgar replied the suffering of five hundred years was on its face. "I have been on Riga for fifty years. I have never seen another of my species. Riga is a planet for transients. I need a home." It stopped, looking down at the ground. "If you had been sure I would have asked if I could come with you." Then it was gone.

Edgar left Riga the next day.

We Eat Pigs, Don't We?

Peter Allen's territory was the galaxy. He had been a prospector for ten years, ever since he was eighteen; now he had his own ship and was his own master. It was true that his ship was a slightly ancient converted ramjet, and that his equipment wasn't particularly modern, but he made it do. He had no ties, no desire to get rich and was in no hurry to go anywhere in particular. And if sometimes he mourned the loss of an especially rich asteroid because of his limited mining equipment and tractor beams, the sadness never lasted long: the galaxy was a big place, he was bound to come across something he could deal with sooner or later, and he generally did. He made enough money to keep himself in supplies and his equipment in repair. He also had enough left over when he made planetfall to indulge in riotous living until he got bored; and that never took long.

Peter was seldom bored when he was riding the spaceways and wandering around in planetary systems which had never been charted, let alone exploited by prospectors like himself. He had been surveying this system for a week, long enough to feel that it had potential. It consisted of a Type G sun, five planets and a belt of asteroids which must have been another planet until some cataclysm shattered it. These asteroids interested him most: his instruments detected a wide range of minerals, including a trace of radokillium, the most valuable and sought-after heavy metal in the galaxy. Just one gram of radokillium could keep a spaceship operating for six months.

Finally Peter had checked all his equipment and was ready to venture into the asteroid belt. He did so cautiously: with his outdated ship one thing he didn't need was to be caught unawares. Eventually he got close enough to bring his most accurate detectors into operation, and the most tedious, yet exciting, part began: scanning each asteroid minutely to get a breakdown of the minerals it contained. He might have to scan a hundred before he found one which was commercially viable. This time, however, he was lucky. He had been scanning only ten minutes before he hit a beauty. He couldn't believe his eyes when he looked at the instruments: this one was full of radokillium, choked to the seams — more than enough to keep his ship moving for a thousand years. A hurried recalculation — more like a *million* years. The thought struck him that it was strange to find such an immense concentration of radokillium in one asteroid, but it was buried in his excitement. His hands shaking, he aligned his tractor beams to harness the asteroid. He forced himself to take his time over the delicate calibration: this was one which wouldn't get away. And when he arrived in the Solar System with this gorgeous thing in tow . . .

Suddenly all the instruments went haywire. He had no time to react before a sun exploded inside his head.

Something was tickling his nose. He opened his eyes and saw a butterfly with steel-blue wings sitting on the tip. He stared at it cross-eyed with astonishment and snorted; the butterfly fled. Still lying on the ground he looked around: he appeared to be in a grassy clearing surrounded by purple trees and bushes; the sky overhead was blue, and — he sniffed in surprise — the air was sweet and warm. He was either on a planet that was suited to his species or he was dead; he thought about it for a while before deciding that the latter couldn't be true. Gradually he began thinking clearly again. Something preposterous had happened. The last thing he remembered was the explosion inside his head, when he was grappling with the asteroid; now he was here, and he had no idea how much time had passed or what had happened. If his ship had been hit by something and he had been rescued it was strange that his rescuers weren't around.

He sat up hurriedly and explored his body: no sign of injury except for a vaguely aching head. The stubble on his face was no more than two or three days' growth — that told him how long he had been unconscious. He stood up cautiously and looked around the clearing and at the forest: it looked quite unspoilt and forbiddingly uninhabited. And where was his ship? This worried him more than anything else, for some reason; his ship had been his home and his life for a very long time and everything he needed to survive was on board . . . . it occurred to him that he was extremely hungry and thirsty.

He was wearing the clothes he normally wore on board ship: a pair of trousers and nothing else. A quick inventory of the pockets turned up a pocket laser, screwdriver and a boiled sweet. He brushed the lint off the sweet and popped it

into his mouth; and began wandering restlessly around the clearing.

Somehow he had been transported to a planet a long way away from where he had found the asteroid. Whoever had done it had either been malevolent, and the asteroid had been a trap, like a piece of fly-paper; or benevolent — in which case where were they anyway? Peter decided that he would have to be very careful. He wasn't entirely unprotected: his pocket laser, although meant to be used primarily as a tool, was powerful enough to stun; its battery had just been recharged and was good for a while. First things first. He must find something to eat and drink. Once that was accomplished he would see.

The butterfly meant that there was animal

life on the planet. The sun was warm, like Earth's, he thought, and the air was rich in oxygen: he might find edible meat or fruit. Setting the laser at full power he ventured into the forest.

It was dim and cool under the canopy of trees. He walked forward carefully, stopping every few steps to listen. He could hear faint scurryings and once, in the distance, a terrifying roar. He shivered; wished he had eyes in the back of his head and a more powerful laser and companionship and that he wasn't here, of all places. The ground seemed to be sloping upwards and he followed it, hoping to climb high enough to get a view of the planet he was on.

Finally the forest thinned out and Peter emerged into a clearing near the top of a small

hill. More important, directly in front of him was a clump of bushes with heavy red fruit hanging from the branches; ravenous now, he picked off one that looked ripe. Caution fought with his appetite: what if it was poisonous? he had no way of testing, but it looked and smelt mouth-watering and there were seeds scattered around the bushes . . . . at any rate, *something* found the fruit edible. So he bit gingerly into the flesh and waited for catastrophe; when nothing happened he took another, larger bite, then another; with the juice running down the sides of his mouth, he tore off a few more and, sitting on a rock, wolfed them down.

They were absolutely delicious. Six took the edge off his appetite and he began to take an interest in his surroundings once more. The forest, interspersed with clearings, stretched out

around him as far as the eye could see. There was a range of mountains in the distance on his right, and he could hear a faint chuckling closer to hand. That might be water. He wiped his mouth and headed in the direction of the sound. It *was* water: a vigorous spring flowing down the hill. Peter slaked his thirst and lay back with his head cradled in his arms, stomach full, the sun on his face. Notwithstanding his satiety, he felt a vague disquiet: this planet was too good to be true and the unanswered questions were too important. But he was warm and a little sleepy . . . . it seemed perfectly safe here, and after a short nap he would think about what he had to do next.

He was woken by a snarling sound. In his half-sleep he thought it was the drill he used to work ore deposits on board his ship, and tried to snuggle back into his nap; then he realized sickenly where he was and jerked to his feet, laser ready. He was just in time to parry a leap aimed at his throat by a large creature like a tiger with eyes jutting out on stalks and incisors as long as tusks. He flung himself to one side and fired at the blur as it went past him; the laser was just powerful enough to knock it out and it crashed to the ground. Peter didn't hang around. He was on his feet and running before the dust had settled. He didn't stop until he had reached an outcrop of rock which could give him some protection and he crouched down, panting, eyes darting from danger to imagined danger. Any sense of well-being he had felt was completely gone now; it was brought home to him with terrifying clarity that he was on an alien world. It took him a long time to regain his composure and to realize that he couldn't have chosen a more secure fortress if he had tried: the only approach to it was the one he had used and he would be able to stop anything that came near him. As he calmed down his resilience and optimism reasserted itself. He was safe now, and even if there were monsters lurking in the forest he would be able to protect himself with his laser . . . . there was food, water, warmth; all he really need worry about at this point was whether he could find some signs that this planet was inhabited by sentient beings. He had no idea how long the day lasted here, but the sun was low in the sky and it seemed reasonable to stay where he was until the next day. So he made himself as comfortable as he could and, watching the approach warily, waited for the night.

The night seemed to last for ever. Peter's spirits alternately rose and sank; once he sat bolt upright, every nerve quivering, when he heard the same roaring noise he had heard earlier, only much closer to hand. It was cold now, and the only protection he had against that were his trousers. He stood it as long as he could, but decided eventually to leave his fortress for a few minutes to look for wood with which to start a fire. He stood in the entrance, eyes straining to cut through the purple darkness. He could see nothing in front of him and only a few pinpricks of light in the distance . . . . pinpricks of light! He stared harder: they were very faint and wavering; they must be fires, and it was almost certain that he would find intelligence there. The pinpricks were clustered underneath the mountain range he had noticed that afternoon. That's where he would go the next day. Peter quickly gathered an armful of wood and took it back to the outcrop of rock. He used the laser to start the fire and waited impatiently for dawn. The fire was a comfort: the shadows retreated.

At first light the next morning he was on his way. He proceeded slowly, mindful of the presence of at least two dangerous types of animal in the forest. He lost his sense of direction almost immediately as the purple vegetation closed in around him and was forced to climb trees to make sure he was heading in the right direction. Once he was halted by a patch of almost impenetrable undergrowth; he had to use the laser to carve out a path and he grudged every erg of energy he was wasting. He did, however, stumble upon the creature with the terrifying roar. It was a furry yellow pig, digging for roots; when Peter appeared it was more shocked than he was and emitted an ear-splitting noise. Peter burst out laughing: this creature was just too ridiculous to be frightening. It transpired that it was also edible.

As evening approached he judged that he was nearly at the point where he had seen the fires. He moved even more cautiously now: there was no reason to suppose that whoever — or whatever — had made the fires was friendly. At length he struck a path which was more than a mere game trail. He followed it, every muscle tensed for action. The forest gave way to a clearing, much larger than any he had passed through; he dropped down from sight in the undergrowth and examined the scene before him with wonder.

In front of him was a cluster of rude shacks made from wood. There were about fifty in

sight. Tendrils of smoke wafted from the roofs of a few. Two or three of the roaring pigs snuffled in the dust of a fairly large yard, or assembly-point; there were many more in a pen on the outskirts of the village. No sign of life apart from the smoke and the pigs; then a figure came out of one shack with a bucket. It was humanoid and wearing some sort of uniform, tattered but faintly recognizable. The figure began walking in Peter's direction and he stared at it with incredulity. He knew that uniform. It was that worn by the Solar System Space Corps — there was no question. Throwing caution to the winds, Peter jumped up and raced towards the man, yelling his joy. The man stopped dead when he saw this figure wearing nothing but a pair of trousers flying across the clearing. Peter reached him and stopped, gasping for breath, a little embarrassed. The man looked impassively at him as, feeling foolish, he said: "I can't tell you how glad I am to see you! Somehow I found myself on this planet."

He stopped, disconcerted by the emptiness in the man's face. Then the man shrugged, brushed past Peter, saying almost to himself: "Another one. They'll never be satisfied."

Peter stood looking stupidly at the figure walking past him. "But where am I?" he yelled. "It doesn't matter," was the faint response.

Vastly puzzled, Peter watched as the man faded into the forest. Then he gathered up the remnants of his tattered dignity and walked into the cluster of dwellings. Figures had begun congregating in the yard and he stopped in front of them. All human, men, women, even some children, about a hundred in all — and the same emptiness he had remarked earlier was on every face. "My name is Peter Allen. I'm an

asteroid miner from Magellen. Something transported me here and took my ship." He hesitated when the congregation remained silent. "Who are you?"

A pause, then a girl, who must have been about Peter's age, spoke. "I'm Brill. Every one of us got here the same way as you did. You're welcome, for what it's worth. Would you like something to eat?"

She turned away and walked into a shack before Peter could reply. The other people began to drift away, all except for three children, who stared at him curiously. He stood irresolute for a moment, then angrily followed Brill.

The shack was cool and dark. Brill was doing something at an open fire in the far corner and spoke as Peter entered. "Don't be angry. They're all good people here. They'll tell you all you want to know in their own time. Sit down here."

She placed a steaming bowl of meat in front of him. Peter's hunger conquered his anger and curiosity for the moment and he ate. Brill watched him without expression. When the edge had been taken off his appetite he began to bombard her with questions.

"Who are you?"
Brill smiled wryly. "You could call me an oyster or a truffle."

"What do you mean?"
No answer.

"What's the matter with everyone here?"
"Nothing much."
"Is this some sort of colony?"
"No."
"How did you all get here?"
"No-one knows."
"But you must have *some* idea?"

26

"Yes. But I won't be the one to tell you."
"Why not?" Brill didn't answer. She walked to the window and looked out at the deserted evening. The sun was setting over the mountains. "Brill — what did you mean when you said 'you're welcome, for what it's worth'?"
"Exactly what I said. If you've finished I'll go out to do some chores. You can sleep here tonight."

That was it. Brill wouldn't answer any more questions. She went out and Peter was left to brood on the little he had learned. It was clear that there was some terrible secret being kept from him. It couldn't be some sort of disease — almost all the people he had seen were extremely sleek and well-fed and healthy, although he had seen a couple who were relatively emaciated. It all tied in with the fact that everyone here had been transported to this planet without volition. And he had seen no signs of activity apart from what was necessary to keep alive — yet all these people came from highly civilized society — and the air of despair in the village . . . . He gave up in disgust and wandered out of the hut.

He explored the village in the gathering gloom. He met a number of the inhabitants, who ignored him with something approaching indifference — and he noticed that they ignored each other as much as possible. After a while Brill joined him and walked with him in silence, except when they passed a man, who was just skin stretched tight over bone, squatting lackadaisically in front of a shack. Brill commented caustically, "He thinks he might escape if he starves himself." Peter asked, without much hope, for elaboration, and wasn't surprised when he received none.

By the time the last of the light was fading from the sky and the purple darkness was descending, they found themselves on the edge of the settlement. A short, thick-set man was preparing a fire. He had piled a large amount of wood together and was now shredding a log into kindling. Peter watched abstractedly, his thoughts far away, conscious of the oppression in the village. Then the man lit the fire, saw that it was burning fiercely — and stepped into it. The smell of burning flesh assailed Peter's nostrils, he yelled and started forward to pull him out. Brill restrained him. "Let him burn," she said. "It's what he wants. He's been here five years now and he can't bear the waiting any longer."

"But why? What do you mean?" cried Peter.

Brill didn't answer, just watched as the rest of the settlement appeared and grouped themselves around the burning man. The fire began to die and the shadows of the people around it danced with a life of their own.

Peter couldn't sleep that night. As he tossed and turned he heard a soft weeping coming from Brill's bed. He moved across the room and took her hand, trying clumsily to comfort her. She gripped his hand fiercely and drew him onto the bed. She held him very tight, making his body shake with the force of her sobbing. He made soothing noises and at length her weeping ebbed.

"Thank you."
"That's OK. Why were you crying? Was it something to do with the man burning himself to death?" Peter asked.

He could feel Brill smiling gently beside him. "It's connected. You see, he was right. After five years it can happen any time, any day, any hour."

"*What* can happen?"
"I'm sorry, Peter. I can't tell you. It's the only way we can make it bearable — not to talk about it, to ignore it, to grow shells around ourselves — it's the only way we can get through each day. Some people decide not to wait. Like John — he's the one who killed himself." She laughed bitterly. "Others try to cheat by starving themselves, or hiding in the forest. It never works." Brill paused, then continued, with heartbreak in her voice: "We even raise children for them!"

She was quiet. Peter stroked her hair and listened to the night. Once a pig roared. Brill stirred. "The pigs have no defence apart from their roars. We don't even have that. I've been here seven years, Peter. I'm valuable, I can bear children. But it has to end sometime. Hold me — don't leave me tonight."

Late the next morning Peter heard a vast humming sound coming from the sky. He looked up, squinting into the brightness, and made out a silver speck dropping rapidly down to the ground. A ship! He grabbed at Brill. "Look!" he cried. "We're saved! That's a —" He stopped when he saw the look of complete terror on her face. "Oh God, they've come! It's my turn now — I know it!" She gripped Peter's arm, her nails digging into his flesh. "What are you talking about? Who are they? What's happening?" Peter asked. Brill, eyes riveted to the ship as it settled into the clearing, answered in a monotone: "Those are our keepers. We

never know when they're going to come. They took twelve of us last time. It's my turn now, I know it, I know it —"

Suddenly Peter found himself unable to move any part of his body except his eyes and mouth. He looked frantically around: everyone, Brill, the man trying to starve himself, all the children were struck the same way. A keening tore at the air. Peter discovered he was screaming — but was impotent to do anything but watch as a ramp was lowered from the ship and four strange, gorgeously-coloured creatures, dragging a trolley behind them, descended. They looked like jellyfish, and they glided over the ground without a sound. They split up and examined every human in turn, very carefully: Peter too, scrutinized clinically by one enormous impersonal eye. Then the aliens seemed to confer and come to a decision. They made for the man who had tried to starve himself, picked him up and loaded him onto the trolley. A little girl was next. The Corpsman, Peter's first contact here, was added to the load. Then a woman, and another. The aliens walked right past Peter and Brill and took away two more men. Seven in all. That was enough, it seemed; they glided back to the ship with the fully-laden trolley. One of them reached inside and threw out a large sack. Then the ramp slid back into the ship and, in total

silence save for the humming, the craft vaulted upwards and was lost to sight.

The paralysis left Peter. Dazed, he looked at Brill and was shocked by her pallor and shallow breathing. She was murmuring in an undertone, "I won't wait for the next time . . . I won't wait for the next time . . . I won't wait for the next time . . ." Peter shook his head to try to clear it and walked over to the sack which had been abandoned by the aliens. He untied the cord around its neck and looked inside. What he saw made him reel back with an inarticulate scream. It was full of bones and human skulls.

Brill walked over to where he was standing, trembling. She had recovered; the mask had dropped over her face again, and her voice was almost studious.

"Yes. Like oyster shells. And they make sure we're in good condition. There's plenty to eat here, and few dangers. The lucky ones are people like John."

Gradually the truth sank in. Peter felt a sick despair and anger settled over him and he kicked at a pig that was snuffling around the sack. It fled, roaring, towards the pen.

"But it's so wrong — so cruel!" he cried out in anguish.

Brill looked at him with a terrible emptiness in her eyes, then at the pig running away.

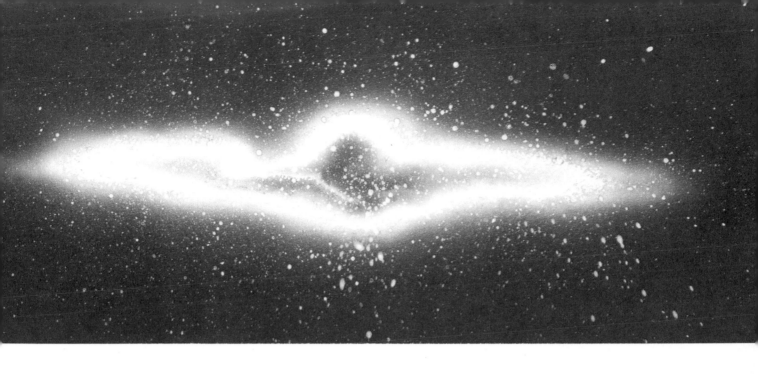

Child of the Graveyard

Intergalactic travel has been achieved. It is now possible to jump from galaxy to galaxy, and from star to star within each galaxy. The Universe has been opened up and is giving up its secrets. Wonder is retreating: there are few surprises any longer.

The major factor that made this possible was the discovery, thousands of years ago, of hyperspace travel and, more recently — about 500 years ago — of wrinkles, for want of a better word, in the fabric of the Universe. These wrinkles are called Gates, and a ship going through one of them can pass from one galaxy to another almost instantaneously. The Gates are situated at the poles of each galaxy, in the heart of a neutron star. Naturally they are of immense strategic value but, paradoxically, the discovery of these wrinkles has made the concept of war and the domination of one species over another impracticable: because of the nature of hyperspace travel — when a ship can leave one point in the Universe and arrive at another point only a few minutes later, and in total surprise — no galaxy can be defended any longer. When the wrinkles were first used there was a burst of cosmic violence which annihilated entire galaxies and wiped out many sentient species; it became clear very soon, however, that it was impossible for one species to take control, and that if the warfare did not cease the entire Universe could be destroyed. Since then there has been peace. A Central Government, which incorporates all sentient species, has been established. All recorded knowledge has been programmed into a Central Computer. The golden age of the Universe has begun. There's only one snag — there's no privacy any longer.

C15 is an insignificant planetary system at one of the poles of the Milky Way. It's so inconspicuous and useless that it merits no more than a number on the galactic maps. The planets orbiting around its Type G sun are totally barren and desolate and the traces of minerals that are present are uneconomic to work. C15 has two distinctive features, though: it is within spitting distance of a neutron star which contains a Gate and, because of its proximity to the star and a bizarre arrangement of planets, it has the strongest gravitational tides anywhere in the Universe. This in itself would be no more than a scientific curiosity and navigational hazard except for one phenomenon — over the millennia every scrap of space debris, every abandoned spaceship, ramjet, shuttle or satellite ever to have been launched in the Milky Way has eventually drifted here. Billions of metres of space are choked with the hardware of a thousand species: some of it so old and obscure that its function can only be guessed at; some relatively modern, dating mostly from the wars that followed the discovery of the Gates. Because of the horrific stresses imposed by the gravitational tides and the cluttered space between the planets very few expeditions, scientific or otherwise, have ventured into the system. Until quite recently.

The discovery of the Gates sounded the death-knell for Humanity. Ten bitter years of war with the Denebians resulted in the almost total obliteration of both species. The remnants of Humanity retreated to what was left of the Solar System and to remote parts of the Milky Way. Homo Sapiens ceased to play a major part in the burgeoning Civilization of the Universe and only the most tenuous links were maintained with Central Government.

One such refuge was C15. Succeeding

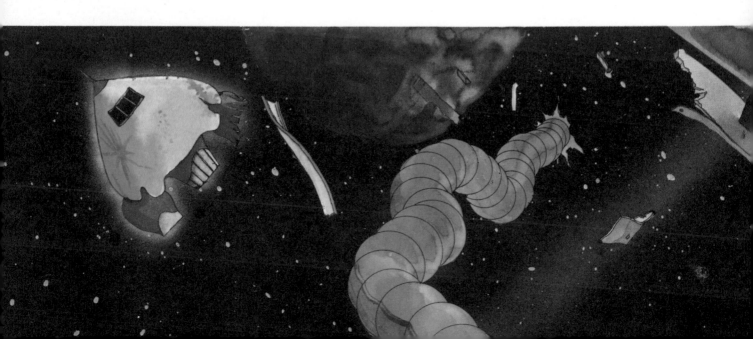

generations of Humanity, depleted even further by the rigours of the life they had chosen, survived precariously in the system. Gradually they began to evolve a civilization of sorts — based on scavenging. A modest trade in artifacts from the Graveyard, as C15 was familiarly named, was developed with the Central Government in return for essentials which were unavailable in C15. Two quirks of personality made Homo Sapiens eminently suited to this life — a xenophobia bordering on paranoia — a legacy from the wars which almost wiped out the species — and a spirit of recklessness which defied logic. The xenophobia extended to the point where Humans shunned each other's company as much as possible: the only times Humanity ever got together in the Graveyard in numbers larger than a family unit were during the Conventions every 10 years. The recklessness was almost necessary — what other sensible species would actually *live* in one of the most dangerous parts of the Universe?

Lara Anders was such a scavenger. She was 22 years old, slim, 1½ metres tall. Her skin was sunburnt almost black and she wore her hair economically short. She dressed practically and skimpily, when she wore anything at all: she had not seen any other Humans since her parents had died in a collision with an abandoned hulk five years before. After an initial period of loneliness she had grown to welcome her solitude.

Lara received supplies every six months from Central Government robot ships and paid for them with scientific curiosities dug out of the wrecks around her. She lived comfortably in a converted cruiser which had been her family's home for four generations. Her only contact with civilization were the robot supply ships, a slightly irascible computer which was linked with the Central Computer, and her collection of tapes. That was all she needed. She was content to ride the gravitational tides in her flitter and to rely on her instincts and navigational aids to keep herself alive.

Time passed and Lara flittered over her territory, turning over the driftwood on her private beach. She spoke only to her computer, to get verification of the finds she made. She argued with it sporadically when she got tired or angry. Once a week she broke out a bottle of Aquavit and sang along with her tapes of classical favourites as they told her of concepts she understood only dimly: love, the moon

rising, summer wine . . . before she drank herself senseless. She didn't miss human companionship at all. In two years she would go to the Convention to choose someone to share her life with: that was tradition, and necessary for the propagation of the species; nevertheless, even now she felt a twinge of resentment at the future disruption of her solitude.

Lara was fazed by only one part of her territory. This was the depths between the sun and the neutron star, where the gravitational tides of the Graveyard were strongest and where her parents had died. But bad memories fade and she made a cautious sortie there. Almost at once, as she swung out around the sun, her instruments told her of a massive body in front of her, perilously close to the neutron star. She edged closer until she could use her scanner. The image was weak and distorted because of the immense forces surrounding the star. The body was an immense spaceship, the biggest she had ever seen, shaped like a disc; on each side were outrigger-like extensions, any one of which would dwarf her home cruiser. She queried her computer, which replied peevishly that it had no data fitting the description supplied by the instruments. This wasn't a surprising answer — so many forgotten species had left relics in the graveyard. The spaceship was also far too close to the neutron star to allow her to examine it too carefully; so, after recording its position, she prepared to leave. She examined it one more time and, on impulse, activated the life-detection instruments. It came as a stunning shock when they indicated that there was a life-source on board.

Lara stood, irresolute, staring at the instruments. Her computer chattered angrily, telling her that it had no records which fitted the data it was receiving. That in itself was shattering: her computer had access to all Central Computer's records, and it had been nearly 200 years since a new life-form was discovered. Lara's latent xenophobia surged; she fought down the desire to leave immediately. She had no sense of duty except in connection with her own species, but she was blessed with a well-developed sense of curiosity. Against her better judgement and the hysterical warnings of the computer she took over control of the flitter and began jockeying it closer to the spaceship.

The flitter inched forward, fighting the gravitational waves and the fury of the neutron star. Lara marvelled at the technology which

would enable the alien spaceship to remain steady in the maelstrom. Soon she could see it with the naked eye. It gleamed dully in the starlight and she fancied she could see a faint nimbus around it . . . Suddenly alarms shrieked out and before she could react the computer overrode her and stalled the flitter.

"Permission to alert Central Government. Emergency status. There is a force-field around the object. There are no records of this type of force-field. There is an 87.3 per cent probability that the object is hostile. Permission to call Central Government before further action is taken."

"Permission denied," Lara snapped out auto-matically, eyes riveted to the instruments. She would not, under *any* circumstances, allow anyone or anything else to help her. Now she knew what the nimbus was and she understood how the spaceship was able to remain so steady. The implications were staggering. A force-field powerful enough to withstand the might of a neutron star . . . the ultimate weapon and the ultimate defence. Whoever possessed this device would be secure for eternity. But — why was the ship here, within the Graveyard? What form of life did it contain? An enormous fear washed over her. What was she *doing* here!

Her hands flew to the controls and nothing. The flitter was powerless.

"Data!" she screamed at the computer,

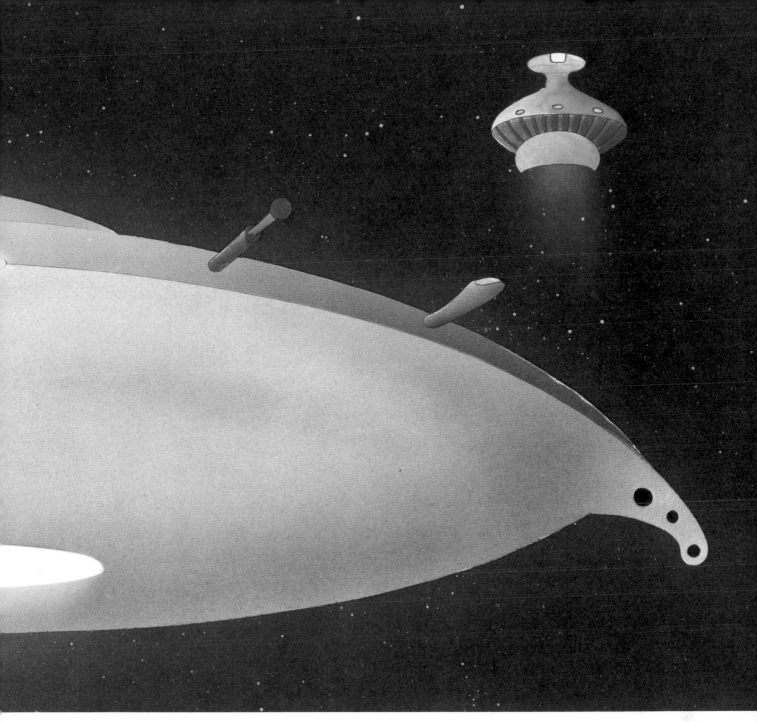

fighting to restrain her panic.

"I have no data. My links with Central Computer are dead," replied the computer heavily. Almost as an afterthought it continued:

"My sensors are picking up signals. They are coming from the object. We are also moving in the direction of the object."

Lara felt as if she had lost the power to move. Terror of the unknown consumed her. Every ancient fear ever to haunt mankind boiled up inside her and she heard herself screaming . . .

And then, all at once, she was calm again. She unfroze and examined the spaceship closely as the flitter approached it. It was almost filling the viewscreen now; the instruments showed that contact would be made on one of the

outriggers. Lara registered at the back of her mind that it was strange her fear had subsided so rapidly and so completely; then her entire attention was concentrated on the outrigger.

As the flitter dropped lower the force-field seemed to ripple. Then it was through the envelope and the gravitational stresses, which were such a normal part of Lara's life, were shockingly absent. Lara felt nauseous at the transition, and she closed her eyes, fighting to prevent the sickness rising; when she opened them again the flitter had landed, as lightly as a feather, on the hull of the outrigger.

The landscape shown in the viewscreen was devoid of any feature that might relieve the bleak grey smoothness of the hull. The

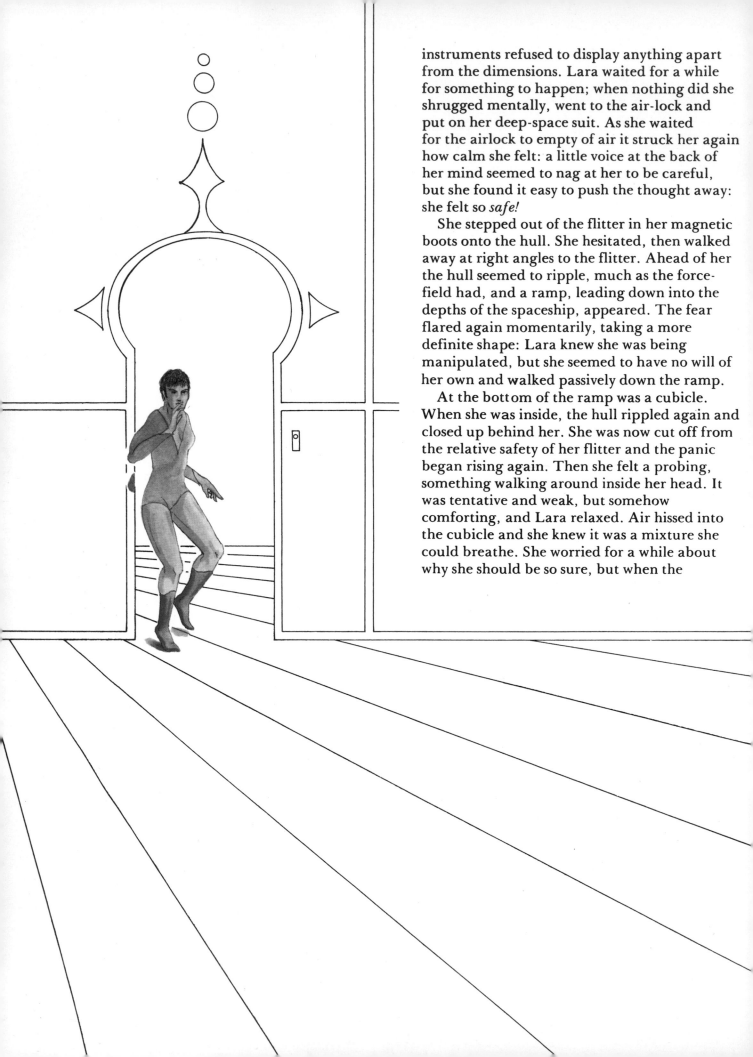

instruments refused to display anything apart
from the dimensions. Lara waited for a while
for something to happen; when nothing did she
shrugged mentally, went to the air-lock and
put on her deep-space suit. As she waited
for the airlock to empty of air it struck her again
how calm she felt: a little voice at the back of
her mind seemed to nag at her to be careful,
but she found it easy to push the thought away:
she felt so *safe!*

She stepped out of the flitter in her magnetic
boots onto the hull. She hesitated, then walked
away at right angles to the flitter. Ahead of her
the hull seemed to ripple, much as the force-
field had, and a ramp, leading down into the
depths of the spaceship, appeared. The fear
flared again momentarily, taking a more
definite shape: Lara knew she was being
manipulated, but she seemed to have no will of
her own and walked passively down the ramp.

At the bottom of the ramp was a cubicle.
When she was inside, the hull rippled again and
closed up behind her. She was now cut off from
the relative safety of her flitter and the panic
began rising again. Then she felt a probing,
something walking around inside her head. It
was tentative and weak, but somehow
comforting, and Lara relaxed. Air hissed into
the cubicle and she knew it was a mixture she
could breathe. She worried for a while about
why she should be so sure, but when the

instruments in her space suit supported her conviction she took off her helmet. The air was cool and fresh; purer than any she had breathed before. She sniffed ecstatically and, slightly drunk with the luxury, took off her constricting space suit. The wall of the cubicle rippled and a long, circular tunnel stretched out in front of her. She entered it, looking around in wonder at the totally incomprehensible machinery lining the walls. She started walking down, away from the outrigger towards the main part of the spaceship.

Presently the tunnel widened out into a huge chamber filled with machinery and instrument consoles. Everything was white and spotless. Lara couldn't hear a sound. She wandered around aimlessly, looking at the dials on some of the instrument consoles: instead of the normal digital calibration measurement seemed to be done by colour. There was something like a rug spread out over the console closest to her and she looked at it with interest: it was a rich brown with red highlights, very fluffy, just crying out to be stroked; Lara didn't. She wasn't going to meddle with anything she wasn't told to.

Lara waited for what seemed like hours. Gradually she became aware of the cold and regretted that she had left her space suit in the cubicle. Eventually she picked up the rug and draped it around her shoulders.

Then she felt a warmth that spread through her entire body. A wash of colours flooded unbidden into her mind. Every synapse of her nervous system responded to the colours as they flowed and shifted; she swayed, her eyes shut in bliss, as they exploded in her brain.

She was in a garden, surrounded by flowers.

She was lying full-length on the grass on a balmy night, looking up at the moon and stars.

She was biting into a peach and her mouth was flooding with flavour.

She was wrapped up in a fluffy towel after a long, scented bath . . .

The images followed each other without pause. They were alien to her, she had no frame of reference for any of them — yet she gloried in, and was consumed by, each of them. She willed them to go on and on and on.

When the pageant ended she found herself lying on the floor with the rug wrapped tightly around her shoulders. She felt a sense of loss, but the warmth was still there as she lay dazed and happy.

"Welcome."

The voice came from inside her head. Lara stirred drowsily, and said, "Thank you." Then, belatedly, "Where are you?" A chuckle sounded inside her head, making her wriggle with pleasure.

"Around your shoulders." *The rug!*

"What are you?"

"I am a —" pause while Lara's memories were riffled —

"— Mother. I was created by the people who built this ship to combat loneliness and to take care of them. They were a very old race, a million years dead before your species emerged. I am immortal, and since my charges died I have been wandering in this ship, learning and reflecting."

"Why did you take control of my flitter?"

"Because you needed me. My purpose is to be a Mother, to take care of those who require care. When you came within range I was saddened by the hurt of your species. That is all ended now. See what I can do for you."

The warmth intensified as the Mother probed further into Lara's mind. She laid bare every fear Lara had ever experienced, then dug deeper and exposed the terrors of her ancestors. When her examination was over she surrounded Lara in waves of comfort.

"Your race are now my charges. I will take care of you. First I shall make us a home."

And the force field leaped outwards, covering billions of metres, enveloping the sun, the planets, the asteroids — and the Graveyard, finally encompassing the entire system of C15; a barrier that was totally impenetrable by any outside agency.

'Now I shall bring all of Humanity here.'

At that moment every Human's mind was linked with every other and with that of the Mother, in complete harmony.

"Now sleep for a while. I will take care of everything." Lara nestled happily into the drowsiness she was feeling. Just before she fell asleep she asked one final question.

"Why did your creators — your charges — die?"

The Mother seemed to hesitate, and then chuckled in Lara's brain.

"Although I have learned a great deal and can now do almost everything they could, that secret still escapes me."

Almost as an afterthought she continued, projecting a vast amusement:

"I sometimes think I might have killed them with kindness."

Taking Care of Baby

The most awe-inspiring feature of the spaceship *Poseidon* was its name. It was a decrepit cargo hulk held together with rubber bands and the prayers of its crew. It was totally undistinguished to look at: coloured a mottled bluish-green, it was shaped like a cross between a hot-water boiler and a codfish. The interior, too, was hardly aesthetically pleasing. The living and working quarters were very cramped, to give as much cargo space as possible. The only recreational facilities were a delapidated table-tennis table and a library. And the food was terrible. Such repairs to have been effected over its two hundred years of service were haphazard, rudimentary and dangerously improvised. But the ship moved, if ponderously; that was all the captain and owner, Xavier S. Nolan, late and unlamented of the Space Corps, wanted. And as a cargo carrier the *Poseidon* was relatively dependable. For twenty years now it had plied between Alpha Centauri and Magellan, and not once had it

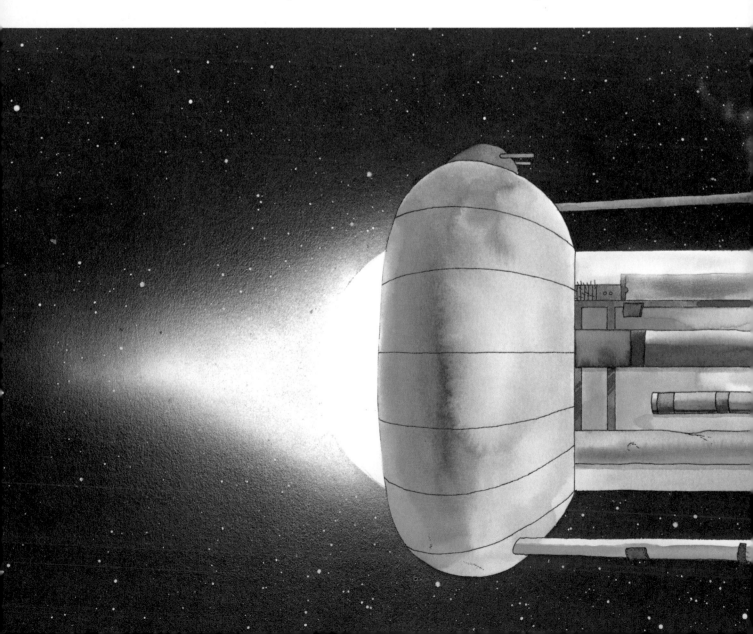

failed to arrive at its destination. It must be admitted that it had arrived late a number of times, once taking six months longer than it should have, but that didn't really count: the *Poseidon* had been involved in an unfortunate collision with a comet which had no right to be in that part of the galaxy at that time of year, and it took a long time to get replacement parts — especially when there was no money to pay for them.

Captain Nolan's crew was as motley as the *Poseidon*'s replacement parts. His second-in-command was a plant from Riga. She looked vaguely like a sunflower, towered over everyone else and moved languidly around on her roots, constantly tripping up the rest of the crew. She was also intensely narcissistic and had a violent temper. No-one except for another sunflower could pronounce her name, so she was nicknamed Grouch. The navigator was a robot called Caruso. Caruso had driven every owner he had had to distraction because of his passion

for opera, particularly Wagner. Nolan had tried to dismantle the robot more than once, because he *hated* Wagner, but was dissuaded each time; beggars can't be choosers, and he had obtained Caruso cheap. Yuk was the engineer. He was a humanoid from the planet Soup in Andromeda: tall and thin and with enormous poetic eyes. He was the only humanoid from Soup in space: this was because the inhabitants of that planet needed more sleep than any other sentient species yet discovered. This made Nolan very unhappy. Yuk was always falling asleep on duty. The ship's company was completed by its defence contingent: two girls from Amazon, very beautiful, called Gog and Magog. They, unfortunately, were terrible cowards.

Captain Nolan himself was short and squat. He had a drinking problem and spent most of his time when he made planetfall drinking in dives. But he also made good contacts there and was able to keep *Poseidon* in more or less

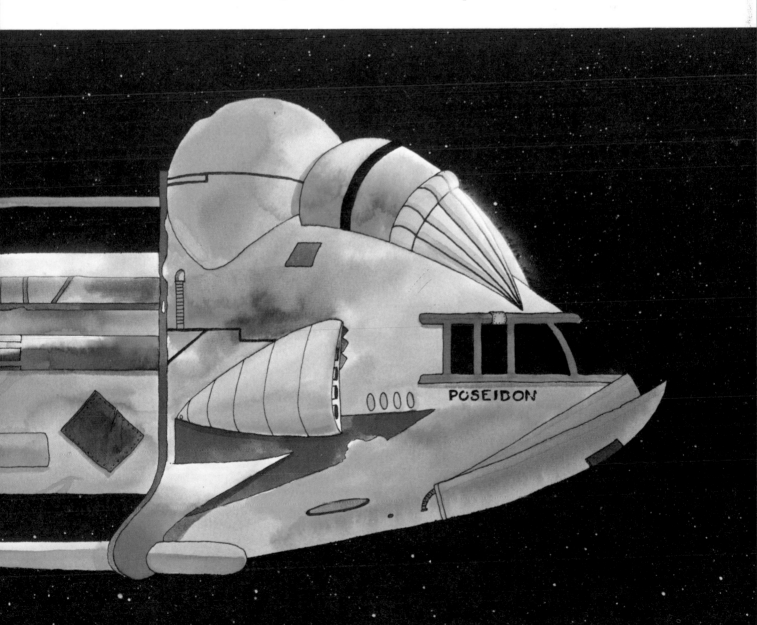

constant employment; and if some of the cargoes were a little illegal, what of it? Money was money. This particular trip the ship was carrying bootleg robot brains from Riga to Earth and had been in space for six weeks. All was well. The engines seemed to be running smoothly, the table-tennis tournament had been won by Gog, Nolan's supply of Aquavit was lasting out and Yuk had fallen asleep only once when he was tending the engines. There was only one snag. They were hopelessly lost.

Caruso, the robot navigator, was the only one who knew it at that moment, and he wondered how to tell the captain, who was sitting in the command chair with a bottle of Aquavit, watching the comets flash by. As was his habit when he was worried, Caruso was singing quietly to himself — *Siegfried,* naturally — and the decision was taken out of his hands when Nolan looked at him irritably, asked him to shut up and to state their position.

"We . . . appear to have drifted, Sir. We are lost, Sir."

Nolan looked a little bemused. "Don't be ridiculous. We can't be lost."

"I'm afraid we are, Sir. You see, I was listening to a particularly fine recording of *The Meistersinger* — it's my favourite Wagner, although *Parsifal* has more drama — and I switched off the navigational apparatus so as not to be distracted from an appreciation of the soprano. It moved me so much, I forgot to switch the apparatus on again. That was yesterday. I've only just discover . . . Now, Captain, don't do anything rash . . ."

Captain Nolan, breathing heavily, shrieking "I can't stand it! I hate you!", was attempting to get at Caruso with a spanner. But the combination of the Aquavit and the robot's avoiding action was too much for him. He tripped over his own feet and crashed to the deck. Gog came running in with Grouch. They examined the captain, who was snoring stentoriously, and concluded that he would live. Grouch assumed command and demanded to know what had been going on. Caruso explained and then ducked behind the command chair as Grouch reacted in the same way as the captain had. The plant was restrained by Gog with some difficulty and in the confusion Yuk came in, rubbing his eyes and complaining that the noise was keeping him awake.

At this point the captain came to and howled for quiet. When relative calm had been established he glared malevolently at Caruso, who was humming unhappily.

"Right. So we're lost. What do you propose to do about it?"

The robot pondered. "I think our best bet would be to get a fix on a star system. Once we have pinpointed its position on the galactic charts relative to our bearing we will have an idea of how far off-course we are. I could then tell you how long it would take to get back en route."

"OK. Get to it. How long will you need?"

Caruso looked at his instruments with some despair. None of the constellations shown was at all familiar. "Perhaps a few days." Nolan looked at his bottle of Aquavit with anguish at this news and then shrugged and went back to his command chair. Grouch folded herself into her seat, muttering ominously as she watched the robot begin the tedious programme of scanning the heavens around the ship for an identifiable star. Gog woke Yuk and the two of them left the control chamber.

Three days later, ship-time, the captain was nursing a hangover, Grouch had beaten Magog up because of a deprecating remark about the plant's appearance; Yuk had trounced Gog at table-tennis; and Caruso had finally worked out their position. The ship had drifted a long way off-course. It would take five days' ship-time to return to their original heading. Nolan looked glumly at the calculations and screamed out for Yuk. The engineer appeared, looking indignant.

"I had just gone to sleep. What's so important?"

"Shut up. This moron here has worked out our position. Look at these calculations. Have we enough fuel to make the course corrections?"

Yuk examined the coordinates, pulled out a slide rule, played with it for a moment.

"No way, Captain. You remember, we couldn't afford to buy more than five milligrams of radokillium when we left Riga. We calculated that it would be sufficient to get us to Earth. Now . . ."

He shrugged his shoulders and looked blandly at the captain. Nolan groaned and turned to Grouch.

"Grouch —" he stopped and looked at the plant. How could a sunflower get a black eye? "—what do you suggest?"

Grouch whirled around to face Caruso. "We can start by dismantling —" She was halted by a rumble from the captain. "Yes Sir. I suggest we

make for the nearest system. There is some possibility that we will find a planet which will yield a little radokillium. We have mining equipment and I can jury-rig refining apparatus with some of our cargo. But it will take a long time to mine enough ore and extract what we need."

The captain's shoulders slumped when he thought of the colossal labour that this would involve. And he was running out of Aquavit. But there was no choice.

"Right, you miserable, off-key piece of tin. Plot a course for the nearest system. And if you wander just once I will personally take you apart right down to the last circuit in your undersized brain. AND DON'T SING!"

Caruso flinched, as much as a robot can. The off-key slur hurt.

Eighteen hours later the *Poseidon* was orbiting a planet which looked completely barren of life. Grouch and Caruso were monitoring the detection lasers, Gog and Magog were looking resplendent in their fetching armoured fighting gear, and the captain and Yuk were asleep. Caruso was singing — *Aida*, for a change — when suddenly Grouch clipped him across the face with a leaf and hissed, "Look! that's radokillium just there or I'm withering. And it's quite close to the surface. Go and wake the captain."

The robot trundled off. Grouch continued to examine the instruments and saw a faint flickering coming from one of the dials. There seemed to be life on the planet: the indications were very faint, and all the other instruments confirmed that the planet was hostile to any known form of life. The plant decided to dismiss the flicker as a malfunction, and by the time Nolan appeared, with red-rimmed eyes and an unbuttoned tunic, she had forgotten. The captain, scratching luxuriously at his stomach, looked blearily at the instruments and said, "Right. We're home and dry. Grouch, take the ship down. Gog and Magog, put on your suits — oh, you're wearing them already. They're very nice — you will do the initial reconnaissance. Caruso, wake up Yuk and tell him to get the mining lasers ready. Then come back here."

Poseidon landed heavily on a flat featureless plain, about a kilometre from where the radokillium deposits had been detected. The airlock opened and Gog and Magog, heavily armed and festooned with equipment, ventured out with a degree of timidity. They looked uncomfortable: understandably so, it was over 500°C out there, and the atmosphere was an unbreathable soup of nitrogen, hydrogen and xenon. They also looked scared: it took an enraged roar over the loudspeakers to send them on their way. Wearing power-packs on their backs, they flew about six metres above the ground. The rest of the crew watched them anxiously through the ship's scanners. A few minutes later Gog and Magog pinpointed the radokillium-bearing rock. Gog chortled when she read her meters. "There's enough here to keep us going for six months! Maybe longer! Captain, there must be deposits like this all over the planet. If we keep its location a secret —"

She broke off when Magog clutched at her arm. The other girl was pointing at a huge oval object a little way away from where they were standing. It was enormous, easily as tall as the *Poseidon*. Although the shape was familiar, those on board couldn't make out any detail.

"Go a little closer," instructed Nolan. Gog and Magog hestitated.

"We'd much rather not, Sir. It's — creepy," opined Magog. The captain groaned in frustration. "Get out there, Caruso," he implored the robot. "Go and hold our bodyguards' hands — don't take that last instruction literally," he added hastily, mindful of his robot's limitations. Caruso, being a robot, did not know what fear was, which made him reckless, and a hideous danger to everyone around him; but he did not need any protective clothing and was with the two girls in no time. The three of them sidled up to the object and circled it cautiously.

"It's hollow, Captain," whispered Magog. "And there's life inside."

Back on board ship Grouch suddenly muttered "Oho" and told Nolan about the instrument reading she had forgotten. Nolan was in a quandry. His trading charter from the Galactic Federation specifically stated that he was not to interfere *in any way* with a new form of life, and was to inform the proper authorities *immediately* — sure enough, this was a new form of life, but think of all that radokillium! Then he realized what the object was: an egg, a whopping great big egg! And if the egg was that size . . . how big would its parents be? For that matter, where were it's parents? Gog and Magog had obviously followed the same lines of reasoning, for they came streaking back to the ship, leaving Caruso staring after them in astonishment.

When the robot got back the ship was in uproar. Gog and Magog were vociferous about leaving before Mother returned; Grouch was losing her temper because of their cowardice, Yuk was brandishing a blaster and the captain was howling for quiet. Nolan finally prevailed and they began considering their options.

"We can't leave. We need the fuel —"

"Yes we can. We can always come back later —"

"Don't be ridiculous. We don't know when the egg will hatch —"

"And suppose its mother comes back and finds us here —"

"Think of all that radokillium —"

" 'What have I e'er remembered yet — but senseless folly dwells in me — ' " — this from Caruso, singing from *Parsifal* — "Shut up, you God-forsaken robot! Be quiet, everyone!" Nolan, red in the face.

It was finally decided that they *would* stay, for just as long as was necessary to extract the

radokillium they needed. Caruso would operate the mining lasers, Gog and Magog would stand guard, Grouch and Yuk would work on the extraction and the captain would oversee everything. Gog and Magog seemed unhappy at this division of responsibilities, but stopped protesting when Grouch looked murderously at them.

The tedious process began: to extract one milligram of radokillium would necessitate moving over a million kilogrammes of ore. The ship's cargo was cannibalized to improvise a reducing plant and Caruso worked like a machine — which, of course, he was. Everything went well. Captain Nolan watched complacently as ore started to pour back to the ship and an incredibly minute proportion of the heavy metal was extracted from each load. At this rate they would be on their way in a few weeks . . . in the meantime, he could not hear Caruso sing, Yuk was too busy to fall asleep, Gog and Magog were gainfully occupied . . . best of all, the egg still showed no signs of hatching.

Three weeks later Grouch informed the captain that enough radokillium had been extracted and that they were ready to go. Nolan had drunk up his entire supply of Aquavit by now and was anxious to get moving; he signalled Caruso in jubilation.

"Caruso — Caruso! Stop singing! Get back to the ship as soon as you can!"

Caruso turned around in surprise. He had been completely immersed in *Lohengrin* and looked around to see who was talking to him, laser still going at full blast. The captain, watching through the scanner, screamed and Grouch went rigid with shock.

"Watch where you point that laser, you dumb robot!" yelled Nolan.

Caruso started when he saw where the laser was directed: for it was bathing the egg, heating it to incandescence, and large cracks were forming over the surface. A huge glistening green foot emerged and began tearing at the shell with enormous efficiency. Gog and Magog paled under their protective clothing and fired at the egg — with no result except to speed up the destruction of the shell. Then the occupant was revealed in all its glory, and the two girls were racing back to the ship, Caruso at their heels. Baby was a gargantuan dragon with an armoured green body and head. It's mouth was open, displaying row upon row of razor-sharp teeth. It had two eyes which extended out from

50

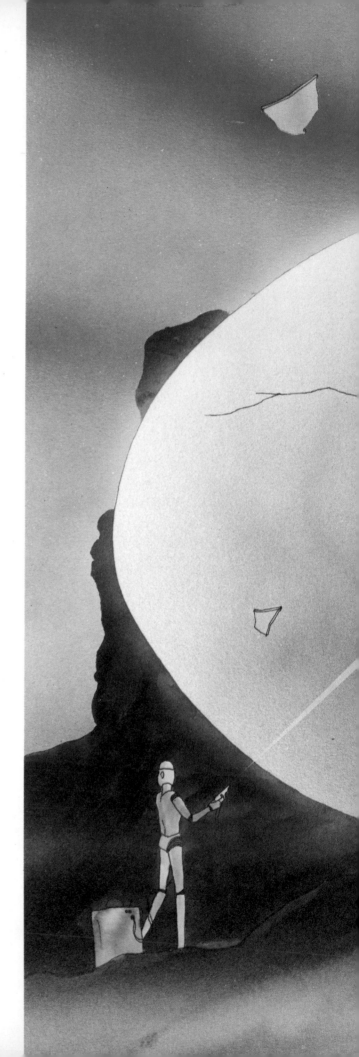

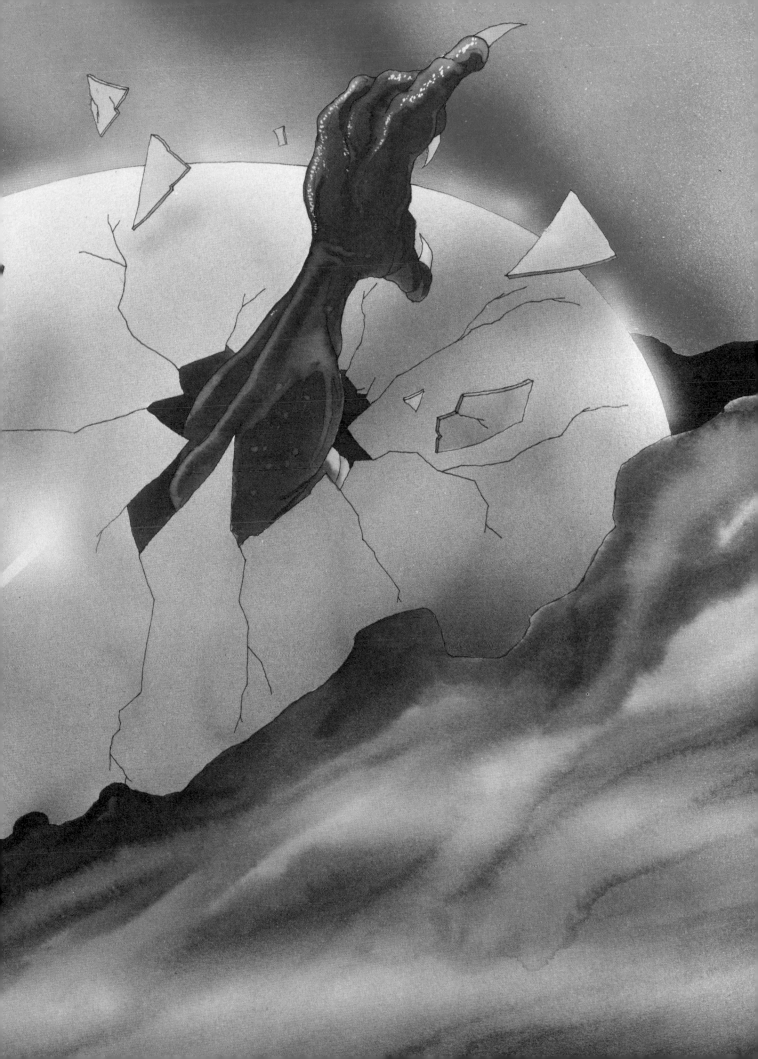

its head on wildly-waving stalks, and a thick, powerful tail which was at least as long as its body and which thrashed around frenetically as Baby staggered to its feet. By this time Gog, Magog and Caruso had tumbled back on board and total pandemonium reigned in the control chamber. Captain Nolan wanted to take off immediately and Grouch concurred, but felt it was her duty to point out that Yuk was asleep and that it would take some time to wake him up and warm up the engines. Caruso was singing lustily in bewilderment and the girls were screaming in harmony.

Baby was fully upright now, and looked around the plain with eyes that were ridiculously innocent. And as full consciousness developed the crew of the *Poseidon* were bludgeoned by a trumpeting scream that cut through the hull of the ship and hammered around in their skulls. Then Baby saw the ship, screamed "XYPHZ!!!!" and leaped towards it, landing on top with an immense thump. It scrabbled around, tearing at the dome directly above the control chamber, obviously intent on taking the *Poseidon* to pieces — or was it? For as they watched, totally deafened by the noise, on the scanners, the monster saw the exhaust pipes for the engines and clamped its mouth over them. When nothing issued — the engines had not been turned on yet — Baby scrabbled harder and let out the loudest caterwauling yet. Nolan stumbled to the controls, hands held over his ears, face contorted in agony. He switched on the engines, hoping to blast the creature off the ship. As the motors warmed to their work and a stream of superheated ions exploded from the exhaust pipes, Baby quietened. Then it plunged its mouth over the pipes and drank greedily. Nolan and his crew watched in stupefaction, and then in despair as the fuel indicators signalled the draining away of every erg of power before anyone could do anything about it. Finally, having sucked the exhaust dry, Baby was, blissfully, silent, and the crew could hear themselves think.

"That's it."

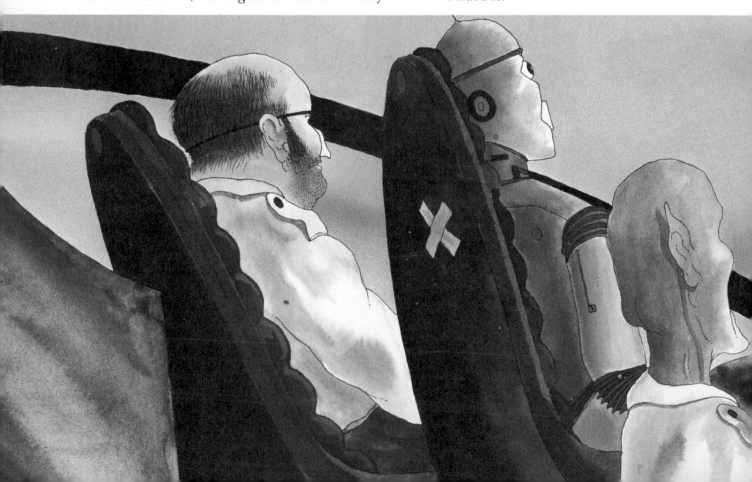

"Yes. We're sunk."

" 'Dead together! All are dead!' " Caruso, from *Tristan,* occasioning a blow with a spanner from Grouch; the robot went into a sulk, refusing to play any further part in this conversation.

"Don't talk rubbish. All we have to do is to kill the creature, find more radokillium and we'll be fine —"

"And how do you propose to kill the creature? —"

"And suppose its mother comes back —"

"We don't even know if there is a mother —"

"And if the Galactic Federation ever hear of it —"

"I'd like to go to sleep now if I may, Sir —"

"You go to sleep, and you'll never wake up again. I'll make sure of that —"

"Oh God, it's starting again —"

And sure enough, Baby had woken up, and was feeling lonely. An immense wail split the air and all the crew except for Caruso clapped their hands (or leaves) over their ears in anguish. Then Gog, of all people, had an idea.

"Captain, I have an idea," she screamed. "Why don't we get Caruso to sing it a lullaby?"

Nolan looked at her in disbelief. Then with the air of a condemned man willing to try anything, he rapped Caruso on the head and shouted, "Sing a lullaby over the external loudspeakers!"

The robot nearly had a seizure in his brain circuits. The captain wanted him to sing?

"You want me to sing?"

"Yes, Ohmigod, can't you follow the simplest instructions?"

Caruso was delighted. He activated the external loudspeakers and paused in reflection: what would be most appropriate, Brahms' *Lullaby,* a soothing little something from Verdi — or would the creature appreciate a touch of Wagner? Or . . . he saw a truly homicidal expression come over Nolan's face, and hurriedly launched into the *Lullaby.*

And it worked. Baby stopped wailing. Nolan twitched in frustration as he listened to Caruso sing, but there was nothing he could do. And when the robot finished the lullaby the silence was heavenly. But they were unable to savour it for long, for the planet seemed to shake and one glance through the scanner confirmed the worst: a reproduction of the baby, only twenty times bigger and more ferocious-looking, had landed on the plain. It was unquestionably Mother, for she looked at the remnants of the egg and then at the spaceship, with Baby apparently expired on the hull; and with the light of pure murder in her eyes she was at the *Poseidon* and snatching Baby up to inspect for damage. A quick once-over and a joyful scream from Baby was enough to convince her that her offspring was alright, and she turned her attention to the *Poseidon*

"WHXYTITHZPHILLOSQB?" she asked.

The crew reeled from the sheer volume of her question and looked at each other in blank incomprehension. Then Nolan had had enough. This was the absolute end. He had never been in such a ridiculous situation in his life and, By God, he was going to give this refugee from a comic strip a piece of his mind. He flicked on the outside intercom, turned up the volume as far as it would go and screamed: "THAT'S IT, YOU OVERSIZED COW! WE FEED YOUR BRAT, WE SING IT TO SLEEP, WE TAKE CARE OF IT — IF I WERE OUTSIDE I WOULD —" and the intercom shorted out.

The mother monster looked slightly taken aback at this outburst, and when her child murmured "XPHZ" to her, she seemed to understand what had happened. She looked at the *Poseidon* with an expression as close to apology as a monster could get on her face, clutched Baby to her incredible green armoured bosom, and vaulted up into space, to be lost from view in a couple of seconds.

The crew of the Poseidon were very quiet for a while after the dragons had departed. Then Nolan roused himself wearily. "Right. We're back where we started. Caruso, get out there with the mining lasers and dig up some more ore. Grouch, set up the reducing plant. I'm going to bed. And if I hear a single word about any of this from anyone — and if you sing in my hearing, Caruso — I will abandon you on this benighted planet. Now get to work."

The Talent

Three weeks after his fourteenth birthday Russell heard whispers inside his head.

They were faint: almost insubstantial, like the remnants of a dream after breakfast, and easy to dismiss. Russell enjoyed listening to music and often had tunes rattling insistently inside his head — to the point when he felt like howling in frustration; these whispers were obviously a more unobtrusive variation on the same theme. Besides, he had other things on his mind.

Russell was born on Ganymede. For the last three generations his family had been asteroid miners. Then, when he was ten, came disaster. His father and two uncles were killed when mining charges exploded on board their ship. Russell and his mother, Anna, were the only members of the family left alive, and Anna took the highly debatable decision to go back to Earth. She spent almost all their money on passage, and they were forced to live in one of the more dangerous neighbourhoods in the urban disaster area that was modern New York. They survived, with some difficulty: New York, in common with most large cities left on Earth, was now an extremely perilous place in which to exist. When interstellar travel finally became a reality, Earth's population problems ended: homo sapiens left the planet in droves for other, less exhausted systems. Most of those who stayed behind abandoned the cities for the countryside and those grotesque, sprawling conurbations which had been the hallmark of the over-populated 23rd Century fell into decay. They became the last refuge of the dispossessed and the outcast, and were scourged by gangs of criminals and, in the case of New York in winter, roving wolf-packs.

Russell was eleven when they arrived in New York. Because he had been born and brought up on Ganymede his physique was strikingly different from that of the boys around him: he was tall and slight, undermuscled in comparison; he was also sunburned to a rich brown, had golden eyes and a head of wispy white hair. His appearance in conjunction with his shyness made him the natural target of huskier boys his own age: consequently he had developed a fleetness of foot which generally kept him out of trouble. But not always. Two minutes after he had heard the whispers he was surprised by a group of boys and girls. They surrounded him so that he couldn't escape and, taunting him and shrieking with laughter, stole his clothes. Then they rubbed his face in the mud and after kicking him a little half-heartedly, disappeared. When they had left he waited until it was dark and scurried back to the two rooms he shared with his mother, seething with the humiliation. The whispers didn't get another thought.

Russell and his mother lived in a fortified square in the heart of New York. The Square was called the Fortress, and it was exactly that: reinforced walls and guarded roofs, with men patrolling the perimeters in a state of constant readiness. Living like this in the cities was the

only way of preserving social values, offering, as it did, the best chance for a family to stay alive and together. There were fifteen families in the Fortress: a total of eighty people including children. The acknowledged leader was a huge, hairy ex space corps officer called Arran who loved children. He had an especially soft spot for Russell, perhaps because of the boy's slightness. Russell admired him to the point of adoration.

The Fortress boasted a school — albeit a rudimentary one. Russell was in his element in the classroom. He had an excellent memory and a flair for mathematics. The teacher was Arran's wife, Lillian. She fostered his intelligence jealously, like a rose-grower with a rare bloom, and had high hopes that he would attend the university in Portland — the only one left on the American mainland. Fifteen other children attended the school, including Russell's tormentors. The attention he received from Lillian was probably the most immediate cause of their attack on his dignity. As always, he kept out of their way as much as possible, and pretended the ambush had never happened. It made for a lonely life; but he didn't mind too much. He loved reading in the library and listening to music in the communal hall, and if he needed human company there was always his mother, or Arran, or Lillian.

One month after the attack, Russell was sitting with his mother in the living-room. It was evening; Anna was mending a tear in a sheet; he was sprawled out on the floor, reading. Neither had spoken for a long time. Anna was absorbed in her thoughts, Russell in his book. A normal domestic evening, until Russell suddenly sat up, head poised as if he was listening to something.

"Mother, there's someone talking."

Anna looked sharply at her son. No-one was near the room.

"You're imagining things. There's no-one here except us."

"No, really, mother." His brow furrowed in concentration. "It's like someone speaking inside my head. It's very faint. A man's voice. He's very excited." He stopped and stared at the wall with unfocussed eyes. Anna watched him with growing concern. Then Russell's voice cracked with alarm. "Mother! He's talking about raiding the Fortress! He's talking to many other people — I can hear them now! They —" he broke off in bewilderment, searching for the right words. " — smell terrible!"

Anna was worried now. She had a healthy respect for her son's imagination, but this was the most outrageous manifestation of it yet. She stood up, caught Russell by the shoulders and shook him, breaking his concentration and bringing his eyes back into focus.

"Russell, stop it! There's no-one speaking to you except me! If this is your idea of a joke I don't find it at all funny! Do you feel all right?"

Russell looked at his mother in surprise. "There really *was* someone, and I feel fine! That voice was inside my head — it's no joke! That man —" he ground to a halt when he saw the queer expression on his mother's face. "Why are you looking at me like that?"

Anna looked away, thinking that she would have to speak to Lillian about making Russell work too hard at school.

She got her chance the next day and Lillian promised to let up on the boy. They both derived some amusement at the facility of his imagination; Russell, after a couple of abortive attempts to convince one or the other of them let the matter drop.

Three days later the Fortress was attacked by a gang of thirty men. They blasted down the front gate and got as far as the communal hall before the defenders rallied and beat them off, but casualties were high: fourteen men were killed and two women captured. One of them was Anna. Past experience had proved that there was little point in going after the women.

Russell, not really comprehending what had happened, passed into Lillian's care. When the loss of his mother finally sank in his despair was cushioned by Lillian's coddling. But he remembered that somehow he had known about the attack before it had taken place, and that no-one had believed him, and a change that was visible only in his eyes took place in him. If in the past he had looked at the people around him with a directness that was out of keeping with his years, now his gaze seemed to pierce through to the soul. Lillian also remembered his premonition, if that was what it was, but she tended to treat it as a coincidence; and any change she remarked in her charge she put down to his grief at losing his mother.

She did, however, tell her husband the story. To her surprise Arran took it very much more seriously than she had. He became defensive when she expressed her scepticism and mumbled something about having heard some strange rumours about extrasensory perception

when he was in the space corps. As soon as the opportunity presented itself he subjected Russell to a careful interrogation.

"This voice you heard inside your head — what was it like?"

"I don't know. Like any voice. Only faint, like it was coming from a long way away."

"Has this happened to you before?"

"Uh — yes, a couple of weeks ago. Maybe longer. I heard something then, but I couldn't make out any words — I thought it was music."

"Music?"

"Yes. . . you know, when a tune gets stuck inside your head. . .?"

"Will you tell me if you ever hear these voices again?"

"OK, but —"

"What?"

"Nothing."

Arran left it at that. He watched Russell walking out of the room with the niggling feeling that the boy had not been entirely frank with him. He decided to ask Lillian to watch him like a hawk and report to him if she saw or heard anything unusual.

A year drifted by. With every succeeding day Russell became quieter. He lost a little weight and his eyes glowed brighter. Lillian fussed over him, made sure that he wasn't sickening for anything, but on Arran's advice left him to struggle on his own with whatever was bothering him. Once or twice she caught him pressing at his temples with knuckles which had gone white with strain, and he was becoming increasingly absent in the classroom — which was not to say that his work was suffering, but that he answered questions automatically, as if his mind was elsewhere while he was speaking. . . And he was beginning to show an anticipation which was far beyond that of any normally bright student. This was particularly noticeable when she attempted to teach her class maths. Every student except Russell was struggling to make the logical jump from one stage of an algebraic proposition to another, and the concentration and frustration in the room was tangible. Russell, on the other hand, was staring out of the window, lost in his own thoughts. He had obviously worked out the answer and had dismissed algebra from his mind. On impulse Lillian called out sharply to him, causing him to turn away from the window with a start, and asked him a question which not only had nothing to do with the problem at hand, but was sufficiently abstruse to defeat

even a first-year student at university. Surprise still in his face, he looked at her and came back instantaneously with the right answer. Lillian was staggered. She asked him how he had arrived at that answer and he hedged, looking hunted. "It just seemed like the right answer," he mumbled. Lillian snorted to cover her bewilderment and let the matter drop.

When the class broke up Lillian stayed behind in the room, brooding. It was just possible that Russell was a mathematical genius, but the *speed* of his answer! The only reason she knew the answer herself was because she had memorized the problem when she was at university; not even a computer, she was sure, could have solved it so quickly with no programming.

She told her husband about it. He scratched at his beard and nodded his head dolefully.

"Yes, it fits the pattern," he said. "I think he *must* have some sort of extrasensory talent. It's possible he read your mind."

Arran held up his hand as Lillian began to protest. "Wait. You know how he avoids the other boys as much as possible. Understandably so. They're a rough bunch with few brains between them. Well, a few days ago I was in the lookout tower. I was watching some of the boys preparing an ambush near the school — you know, that game they play, where they jump out and scare the living daylights out of their victim — anyway, I looked around for the person they were waiting for, and saw Russell walking in that direction. And, Lillian, it was amazing. He stopped, looked up at me, then at the vicinity of the ambush. There was no way he could have seen what was in store for him, but he made a detour and entered the school from the back." Arran stopped to judge his wife's reaction. Then he said quietly, "I think he read my mind. He knew what was waiting for him."

Lillian was very confused. She knew her husband was level-headed — he had to be, to be capable of leading the rabble in the Fortress — and not given to speculation. Yet. . . this was ridiculous, and she told him so. Arran grinned and said, "Yes, I know how you feel. But there are other things besides. Look at his eyes. They drill right through you without seeming to notice your presence. And you know how the other children try to torment him. Don't you think it's strange that not once, not *once* since last year has he come even *near* a confrontation? And isn't it strange how he seems to answer you almost before you ask him

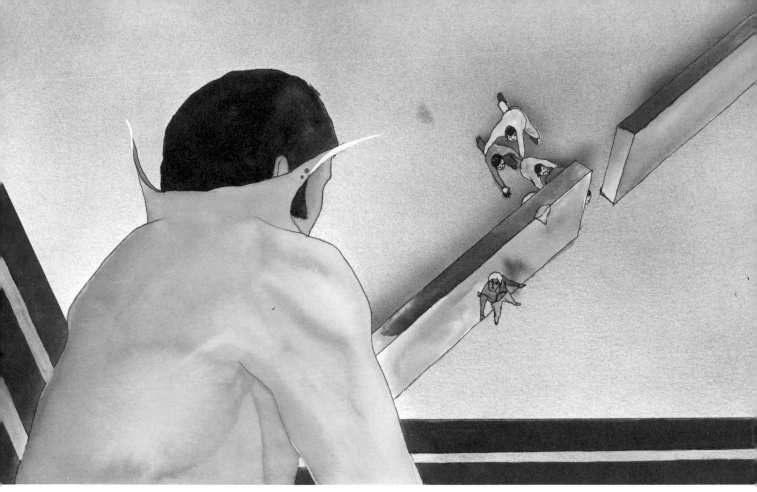

anything?" He sighed heavily. "Well, I'm not about to push him. If he's going to tell us what's going on inside his head it'll be in his own time."

Arran was right. Two days later Russell came up to him with a look of embarrassment on his face. He shifted from foot to foot, avoiding the big man's eyes, and finally spoke.

"Arran, you remember, I heard those voices inside my head last year?" Arran nodded. "Well, I'm hearing them again. The same voices. And this time they're much clearer. A few minutes ago one man — I think he must be the leader — was saying that they should raid the Fortress again. The others were arguing with him. But they're all scared —" he stopped and screwed up his face in concentration. "Arran — Arran! They're going to come tonight, at midnight! I'm not joking! This is like the last time —" he trailed off. Arran looked at him, mind in turmoil. Then he made a decision, ordered Russell to stay where he was and left the room.

When he returned he had Lillian with him. "Right. I've tripled the guard around the perimeter. If they come tonight we'll be ready for them. Now we want to ask you questions. Is that all right?" Russell nodded reluctantly.

Lillian jumped in with the first question.

"Can you read minds? Are you reading mine right now?"

Russell looked at her in despair. "Yes, I can. But since two days ago I haven't been able to read yours. I was in my room and I heard both of you talking about me inside my head. But after that you seemed to — close down your mind." He turned to Arran. "Like you did, just after you warned me of the ambush."

Arran looked at Lillian. "Some sort of mental blocking effect. Once we began to believe he could read minds we put up shutters inside our heads." Then, to Russell, "Can you read the minds of everyone else?"

"Yes. Sometimes one person sounds louder inside my head than another. Like that man outside. And I can turn it off if I want to. I'm glad I can. So many people. . . it's messy. And I feel as if I'm trespassing."

"Can you hear thoughts from some distance away? Say as far as the space-port?"

"No. I think my range is quite short. But it's increasing all the time."

"Does anyone else in the Fortress know about this?"

"No. But the other boys suspect something."

The two adults were silent for a while, lost in the implications of Russell's talent. When Arran shook his head and spoke to the boy.

"We'll have to talk about this again. In the meantime, don't tell anyone else."

When Russell had left, Arran and Lillian tried to work out what they should do. Arran was all for informing the people at the university — they would be able to understand this better than they could. Lillian disagreed. She felt that Russell was too young and she disliked the idea of his being treated as a scientific experiment. It would do no harm to wait a while. Besides, if his talent was reliable, and he was prepared to use it, he would be the perfect early warning system of any trouble which might be brewing . . . At any rate, let him stay until he himself knows what he would like to do. Arran finally agreed, with reservations.

At midnight every available able-bodied man or woman was concealed at strategic points along the perimeter of the Fortress. The attacks on the community had been ruinous, if sporadic, in the past, and Arran was determined to establish the impregnability of the Fortress by annihilating the raiders that night. Decoy sentries were posted in the usual places and everything looked normal; so that when thirty men snaked over the wall and prepared to dispose of the sentries they received a rude shock. At Arran's command the men and women lying in wait opened fire and in less than a minute every raider who had made it over the wall was either dead or dying. The remnants on the other side melted into the night. Arran was content to let them go: they would spread the word about the disaster, and other groups would be properly wary of attacking the Fortress in the future. He looked vaguely around for Russell, hoping that the boy would be able to identify the leader of this particular gang, and was startled to see him curled up in a foetal ball against the wall. He examined him anxiously: he was unhurt physically, but his eyes were screwed shut and his face was contorted horribly in anguish. Arran shook him and slapped his face to bring him around, with no success; he decided finally to put the boy to bed and hope that he would recover consciousness soon. Lillian was in no doubt about what had happened. Russell had been unable to screen out the impact of so many dying minds, and had gone into a state of total shock . . . all they could do now was pray that he recover from the trauma.

It took him three days. When he finally recovered consciousness and opened his eyes Lillian, who was at his bedside, reeled backwards at the sheer torment blazing from his eyes — it was like a physical blow. He screamed, again and again, his body going through impossible contortions. Lillian was powerless to restrain him, and it took Arran and two other men to pin him to the bed and lash him down. Mercifully, he slumped back into unconsciousness in a short while and when he woke up the next day he was calm, but very weak.

The mental scars healed slowly — a month before he could speak rationally again, and another month before he was capable of moving around. And shadows remained: it was almost impossible to meet his eyes, so much pain had they retained. Altogether his convalescence took six months. For most of that time he lay or sat silently, staring into space. Then, late one evening, he gave a shattering demonstration of the new way his talent had developed.

He was sitting with Arran and Lillian. The two adults were reading. Lillian looked up from her book, to see Russell wandering restlessly around the room.

"Is anything the matter, Russell? Can I get you anything?"

"No thanks, Lillian. I'm just working something out." Lillian went back to her book. A paragraph later she looked up in shock. It had taken her that long to realize that Russell hadn't opened his mouth to speak. The words had appeared fully-formed inside her head.

"How did you do that?" she gasped.

"Do what?" said Arran, looking up. The stupefaction on his face was almost ludicrous as Russell expanded the projection of his thoughts to take him in.

"Yes, I can beam thoughts at you now. And I can also do this." — And an outpouring of warmth flooded through their brains.

"Also this."

He seemed to lay open his mind, so that they could see into every corner of his soul. They were drawn in, and swam in the currents of pain and joy and every conceivable emotion Russell had ever felt; when they finally surfaced they felt as if they had been away for millions of years. Then he 'spoke' to them again.

"Arran — Lillian, I don't know what is happening. It's like I was blind all my life and vision is returning. The process isn't complete yet. Something is telling me that I have to go away. I need to go to a place where nothing can distract me. You will not see me again, but I will always be with you."

"Where will you go?" cried Lillian, feeling a sense of loss that was unbearable.

"To the spaceport first. Then I will go into space. I don't know yet what will happen after that."

"But the spaceport is right across the city, on the outskirts! And how will you get on board a ship?"

Arran and Lillian felt a tickle of amusement. "I'll manage. Don't forget I can't be taken unawares."

Then the shadow of a kiss was planted in the middle of their minds and he was gone.

Outside the Fortress Russell reached out with his mind towards the spaceport to get his bearings. The he set out, threading his way through the devastated streets. It was very cold: the middle of January, and the temperature was well below freezing, but he hardly felt it. One advantage was that no-one else would be out on a night like this, but it became clear very soon that he was still surrounded by danger. He heard a long-drawn out howl coming from the buildings on his right. He probed with his mind to identify the sound and realized with a start that it was wolves — many of them, and that they were aware of his presence. Russell had no idea if he could control them in any way, but they were emerging from the buildings and surrounding him. He probed a little deeper and was nauseated by the stench of their hunger and greed. Almost automatically he projected his repugnance, and the wolves stopped dead. Then he flung hatred at them and they scattered, whining in fear. He went on, comforted by the knowledge that he would be able to deal with any more which might appear.

Russell made good time, given the difficult terrain. By daybreak he had reached the space-port, and concealed himself behind a wall. He reached out with his mind, probing to discover which of the spacecraft on the launching pads was ready to go. He quickly made contact with the brain of a rather sleepy flight-controller and established that a scoutship had recently been refuelled and would be perfect for him. A little later he was on board. He was stumped momentarily when he realized that he had not the faintest idea about how to operate the controls, then shrugged and reached out to riffle through the memories of a pilot asleep in the flight-tower. In five minutes he had mastered the techniques involved and the scoutship was blasting through the stratosphere. No-one on the ground had any time to react.

Russell drove the spaceship on until he was out of reach of the Sun's gravitational pull. Then, in interstellar space, he cut the engines, allowing the craft to drift. He was finally out of contact with the maelstrom of minds in the Solar System.

He put on a spacesuit and climbed out onto the hull of the ship. Floating in free space, he allowed his mind to expand, letting down all the barriers, reaching out to the stars. Colours exploded behind his eyes, and, for the first time in his life, someone 'spoke' to him.

"Welcome. We've been waiting for you to join us."

"Who are you?"

"We are thought — consciousness — reality — dreams. We are free. We roam the Universe. We are the Universe.

"Why should I join you?"

"See what we offer."

Visions exploded inside Russell's head. He saw a pageant of galaxies marching brilliantly through space, tearing eternal darknesses away. He felt the tension of creation as matter was formed in the Deeps. He heard the wind ravening over the crusts of newly-spawned planets. And cutting through the visions was a sense of unity and harmony.

"The alternative if you choose to go back to Earth —"

Unity dissolved and Russell saw himself on Earth, battered by the screaming of a million minds, torn apart by the loneliness of being unique. The death trauma returned, multiplied many times, and he felt it drawing him under.

"Join us now."

And Russell decided. His mind wriggled out of his body, leaving the husk to drift forever between the stars. He whirled once, glorying in the freedom.

Into interstellar space, in the galaxy of Alpha Centauri, a new star came into being.

Zoo Story

Rodney was jerked out of a deep sleep by an enraged bellow in his one exposed ear. His head singing, he sat upright in bed, threw a frantic look at his alarm clock: 7 o'clock, and he'd overslept again — and smiled winningly at the towering, snappily-uniformed figure of the head keeper who had roused him from slumber.

"I'm sorry, Mr Newman, I seem to have overslept —" The head keeper cut him short with another bellow. "Get to work! There's half the Zoo to be cleaned out before we open! And if you oversleep just one more time I'll have your hide!" Rodney scurried to the bathroom. He believed Mr Newman's threat.

Two minutes later he was at the lion's cage, sweeping up the night's debris. The lion, whom he had nicknamed Toothy, was sprawled out in a corner, and watched Rodney with vast disinterest. Rodney kept up a running mutter about how he hated his job and loathed Mr Newman and all the peasants who came to the Zoo to gawk at the animals and how he hated the animals for being in cages. . .

Rodney, you see, loved animals. He had taken this job at the Zoo because he wanted to work with them, but quickly became depressed when he saw how living in cages affected each animal. Some of them took to captivity like ducks to water, and spent their day lolling around indolently, accepting whatever treatment humans gave them; others paced up and down, looking in despair at the wide spaces outside their cages; others settled, but their behaviour was distorted; others died.

It was 8.30 before he had cleaned out all the cages in his section of the Zoo. It would have taken him less time if he had not stopped to talk to the tigers, who were gliding interminably alongside the bars of their cage. His conversation with them took the form of a few sympathetic grunts and clicks of his tongue, and a promise of some especially toothsome morsels when feeding time came around. The two tigers confined their responses to a cold glare.

At 8.45 the gates of the Zoo were flung wide and the public started drifting in. It was a warm, sunny day, ideal for animal-watching, and soon there were throngs of people clustered around the cages. Rodney stood in a corner, reflecting sourly that the animals who got the most attention were generally the ones which he found least interesting — the lions, polar bears, elephants and monkeys, for example. No-one paid too much attention to the Père David's Deer, of which the Zoo was the proud owner of two. These deer were extinct in the wild, and there were only about seven hundred or so in captivity in the world. Rodney adored them.

An hour later he gave the animals their first feed. This always gave the spectators a thrill. Particularly when he went into Toothy's cage and fed the embarrassingly tame lion titbits from his hand. He kept his promise to the tigers and flung two large, bloody haunches into their cage. He had just done this, and was watching them tear at the meat, when he felt someone tugging at this arm. He turned around with some irritation — people were always wanting ridiculous information like, are the tigers in the Zoo man-eaters, and isn't it dangerous — and came face-to-face with the most remarkable-looking man he had ever seen.

The man was a light golden brown and excruciatingly thin. He was bald, had a long, narrow face with limpid blue eyes, and his clothes hung oddly on his body. His hand ended in long, tapering fingers — and had no thumb. "Excuse me," the man said in a heavy accent. "What is this place?"

Rodney was astonished. He had thought that everyone knew what zoos were. "Where on Earth have you come from?!" he exclaimed. "This is a zoo! It's a place where you can see animals which have been captured from the wild so that you can look at them! It's an amusement park — a playground — a graveyard — a museum!"

The man looked into the tigers' cage with

distaste written all over his face. "I think it's terrible," he said, and walked away, melting into the crowds.

Rodney looked after him in surprise and some approval. It wasn't often he met someone who felt the same way as he did about zoos. Then a warning look from Mr Newman, lurking by the elephants, sent him back to work. Soon he had forgotten all about the strange man, and was fulminating at the cruelty of human beings — some bright soul had given one of the monkeys a cake of soap to eat and the poor animal was belching suds all day.

The next morning, at roughly the same time, the man appeared again, this time with three little replicas of himself in tow. He went straight up to Rodney and looked at him with his earnest blue eyes. "Will you be so kind as to escort me and my children around the —" he hesitated before completing his sentence. "— Zoo? I know nothing of any of the animals. I will reward you well."

Rodney, intrigued by the strange family, pointed out that Mr Newman, his boss, was the one to ask. The man nodded, asked Rodney to indicate his boss's whereabouts, and going up to him, engaged in a conference which involved

money changing hands. Mr Newman came back to where Rodney was standing flanked by the three children, and indicated regally that he would allow him to escort the group. Rodney thanked him volubly and sarcastically.

The procession set off, Rodney and the man in front, the children jostling close behind. "My name is Curf," the man said. "We have just arrived here and everything is strange to us. Please do not mind if we ask stupid questions." Rodney nodded, relieved that for once he wasn't faced with the prospect of lecturing to people who thought they knew it all. "Pleased to meet you. My name is Rodney. Where do you come from?"

"From a place a long way away," replied Curf, and changed the subject smoothly, asking him what the animals in the cage they were approaching were. From this point on Rodney had his work cut out answering a veritable barrage of questions about all the animals. He dealt with as many as he could, and his curiosity about the innocence displayed by his charges grew by the minute. Especially when he described the plight of the Père David's Deer and Curf murmured reflectively that that was the only valid reason for a place like this.

Eventually Rodney pleaded exhaustion and suggested that they go to the cafeteria to recharge. Curf and the children drank water and watched with fascination as Rodney sipped at a steaming cup of tea. In his turn he decided to pump these strange people gently. "It seems a little odd that you know so little about the animals on display here," he said. "You must come from a very isolated place. Don't you have animals there?"

"Of course we do," Curf replied. "But they are very different species." Rodney was about to ask him for more information when Curf interposed a question of his own. "Rod-ney," he asked, distorting the name delightfully, "I got the impression that you do not approve completely of this place. Will you tell me why you work here and why the — people feel that such a place is necessary?" Rodney noted Curf's hesitation just before 'people' in the back of his mind, but this was his favourite hobby-horse and he was off. He told them why he had joined the Zoo and of his subsequent disillusionment. He raged about the obscenity of having animals which were much happier in the wild on display. He talked passionately about the only reason zoos should exist — as final sanctuaries for animals which had been decimated by human predators. And he waxed eloquent about the vast nature reserves which had been established all over the world, where animals could live in their natural surroundings, unmolested by human beings. He finally ran down, and was glancing sheepishly from one rapt face to another when Curf interjected quietly:

"What would you like to see happen?"

"What would I like — I would love to see every animal not in danger of extinction returned to its natural habitat. I would love to see every nature reserve surrounded by a high fence so that no-one could harm the animals. I would love to see places like this close down!"

He stopped, startled by his own vehemence. Curf looked seriously at him for a long time and then murmured, "Perhaps we could achieve some of those things." He looked quickly around the cafeteria — it was virtually empty: most of the customers had gone out to watch the second feeding. Then he rapped out something in a foreign language to his children and all three of them clamped their hands around Rodney's wrists. He looked down, startled, and opened his mouth to protest: no sound issued.

69

And a paralysis had settled over his limbs; all he could do was move his eyes. He noticed with a growing panic that, like their father, the children had no thumbs, and then he was overwhelmed by Curf's eyes, which seemed to grow larger and more luminous until Rodney felt as if he was drowning in them. . . "We are, as you are beginning to suspect, not inhabitants of Earth. We come from a planet in a system many light-years away. We are tourists, and we are not allowed to interfere in any way with the lives of you humans. But I feel, as you do, that this place — this *Zoo!* is barbaric. And I think we can bend the rules with your help."

His eyes seemed to grow even larger. Rodney felt a splitting pain at the back of his head, then it cleared and a vision that filled him with an almost unholy joy took its place. His appreciation of what Curf was suggesting was quite plain, and the aliens relaxed their hold on him. The five of them sat back in their seats, smiling gleefully at each other.

That night, at about eleven o'clock, Rodney got out of bed and out of the Zoo. He walked to a prearranged spot and was waiting as the spaceship floated down, bathed in moonlight. He embarked, grinning at his fellow conspirators. The spaceship hovered over the Zoo and Curf flooded the entire area with a gas that sent every living creature to sleep. Then the ship sank down to the ground, Rodney pointed out the cages of the animals which would be happier in their natural habitat, and the five of them set frantically to work. When that was complete the spaceship rose again and spurted purposefully away. In no time at all it was hovering over selected spots in Africa, then Asia, then America, then Canada. . . its final stop was the North Pole, and then it returned to the Zoo. Rodney climbed out and turned to say goodbye to the aliens; Curf, smiling, asked: "And what about you, Rod-ney? Would you like to leave this — human zoo?"

Rodney considered, and refused, a little doubtfully. He embraced the aliens enthusiastically and returned to bed.

He was roused at 6 o'clock by the frantic Mr Newman running into the room. "Wake up! Something terrible has happened! Nearly all the animals have been stolen! Ohmigod, what are we going to do?! The Zoo will have to close —"

Rodney sat up and stitched a look of concern across his face, but inside his heart was singing. He wondered in passing whether the tigers had caught their breakfast yet.

Between the Galaxies

Excerpt from Dr Caldwaller's *History of the Galaxy:* "After an initial, painful reconnaisance of the Solar System Man exploded outwards towards the stars. Contact was made with other sentient species, and *Homo Sapiens* was found wanting; the repercussions shook the galaxy. When the dust finally settled, Man integrated: those members of the species who had survived the holocaust melted into the galactic community and divested themselves of the nationalist chains that had nearly proved their extinction. The chains I talk about are those connected with identifying too closely with insignificant planets in insignificant planetary systems. I postulate that this is a historical pattern: that every species in the galaxy has, to a greater or lesser extent, followed the same course as man took. And now, as the frontiers of the Universe are pushed back and the sentient species of this galaxy reach out across the awesome Deeps, this question must be considered: what will happen when — and note I do not say if — contact is made with similar or more advanced galactic civilizations? Will the game be played out yet again?"

When I was a boy growing up on Earth, my one driving ambition was to be a spaceship pilot. Imagine my chagrin, therefore, when, on my fifteenth birthday, I presented myself at the recruitment offices of the Space Corps, and failed the majority of the tests. It seemed that I was too blind, too uncoordinated and stupid to be an effective member of the Space Corps, or so the rejection slip I received implied. The only tests in which I made reasonable scores were those dealing with my empathy rating: apparently I got on rather better with members of other species than the majority of my fellow humans. But that in itself was not enough, and my other scores effectively put paid to my dreams of a career in the Corps. So, being of an intensely romantic turn of mind, I did the next best thing: I ran away to space.

I stowed away on a liner going to the planet Soup and when I was finally discovered it was too late to do anything about me. I was put to work in the ship's kitchens, helping to feed the 500 passengers on board. Then one of the stewards fell ill and I was promoted to cabin boy and waiter. My empathy rating stood me in good stead here. I spilled few drinks and was sympathetic to the woes of many drunken passengers; consequently, when the liner docked on Soup it was relatively easy to arrange for my position to be made permanent. I have been a steward ever since.

The Earth-Soup trip was a milk run and began to bore me after a while, so I transferred to the *Burge,* a cargo-cum-passenger ship which planet-hopped around the Galactic Rim. This suited me better, and the next two years went by in a flash. Then, when I had just turned eighteen, disaster struck. *Burge* was in orbit around the planet Rog, waiting for clearance to land. Normal shipboard routine had been abandoned for the time being and passengers and crew were in the main dining chamber, celebrating the end of the voyage — you know the sort of party: all the passengers are handed certificates which prove that they have traversed the Rim, and everyone, down to the last crew member, gets paralytically drunk. Well, one maniac decided to launch the flitter and go for a joyride; he lost control when trying to re-enter the *Burge* and crashed into the hull. There was an immense explosion and the ship disintegrated. The only survivors were the chief steward and myself. We had gone down into one of the airtight holds to collect fresh supplies of liquor, and when the explosion tore the ship apart the hold we were in was flung clear. We had enough air to keep ourselves alive until rescue came, and we managed to achieve a degree of comfort by making inroads into the bottles of wines and spirits scattered around us. Both of us had great difficulty enunciating our gratitude on being rescued.

As a planet, Rog had little to offer. I mooched around for a while, trying to find a berth on spaceships bound for other, more attractive parts of the galaxy, with limited success: the best position I was offered was that of temporary nursemaid to a family of Nugs. What made this proposition distinctly unattractive was the extent of the family: there were over 300 baby Nugs to be looked after. I was reaching the end of my tether when on impulse I reapplied to join the Space Corps, this time as a steward. To my complete astonishment — and delight — my high empathy rating was instrumental in getting me accepted. I received orders to proceed to Riga, where I would join my new ship, the *Auriga*.

First sight of the *Auriga* took my breath away. It was an enormous ship, fully ten times the size of anything I had ever travelled in. It wasn't particularly beautiful to look at — it had

a bulbous, greyish-white body with extensions and outriggers which owed little to the rules of symmetry, vestigial wings and, in the stern, a heavily-shielded, businesslike-looking bulge which housed a revolutionary power unit — the Dislocation Drive. The little I had heard about the Drive had given me the impression that it was a ravening monster which almost literally tore at the fabric of the Universe as it drove the ship through hyperspace. It was also highly experimental: too dangerous to be tested fully within the galaxy, it had to be perfected in the vacuum of the Deeps, and was reckoned still to have bugs which needed ironing out. I now had a good idea of the *Auriga's* mission. I was to be part of the crew of a spaceship heading out into the most desolate part of the Universe — the Deeps, the yawning gulf between the galaxies, the breeding-ground of entropy. The prospect was daunting.

I reported to the purser, a red-faced, rather portly man called O'Brien. He was affable; commiserated about the loss of my last ship and told me about this particular trip. The *Auriga* was going to attempt to cross over to N201, a galaxy which looked as though it might be similar to ours. The distances involved were quite incredible: once we got clear of the Outer Rim we would have to travel through 7,000,000 light-years of empty space. True, we would be travelling in hyperspace for the most part; even so no-one was completely sure how long the trip would take. The most conservative estimate was about two years. The *Auriga* was carrying a complement of 400 people: 100 scientists, 100 crew-members and 200 soldiers of the military arm of the Space Corps. O'Brien noticed my disquiet when he mentioned the military, and laughed.

"This is the first time anyone has attempted an expedition of this scale. Who knows what we may come across in N201? Also, the Central Government has an eye to expansion: this galaxy is getting a little crowded. And the military will make that easier."

I was also briefed on my duties on board ship. In addition to being a steward I was to act as loose liaison among the three groups of passengers. This was reasonable: the scientists' antipathy towards the military and vice-versa was well-known, and in my capacity as one of the stewards I was in a position to mix freely with members of both camps. I met my immediate superior, the chief steward, Kelly B'Nath: a furry, highly sympathetic squid from

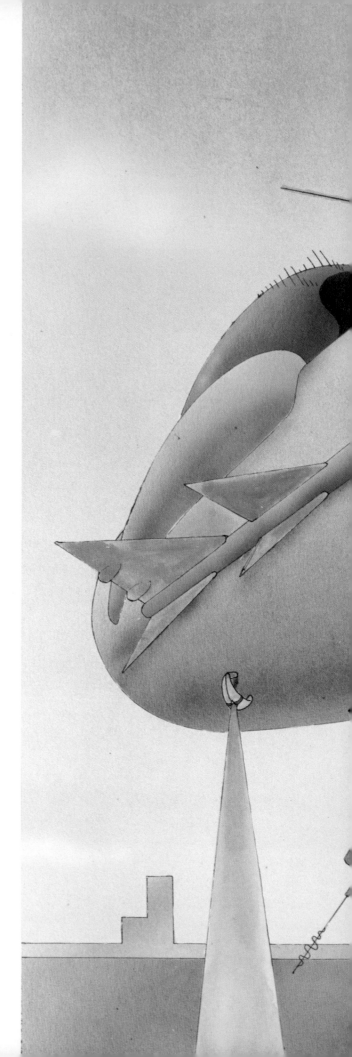

Antares. I was to share a cabin with two other stewards, a ferocious-looking Andromedan called Phyll, and a squat humanoid from Ivory. His name was Gorg, and he had one eye.

The *Auriga* took off. It travelled at a stately pace through the populated regions of the Outer Rim, using conventional hyperspace power. I was kept busy ministering to the needs of space-sick scientists and keeping a division of soldiers fed and watered, and I hardly noticed the shift into hyperspace. It was, after all, something I was quite used to: the sudden nausea and feeling that everything had gone translucent were a normal part of my life. It was different, however, when the *Auriga* had

reached the edge of the Deeps and the Dislocation Drive cut in. Everyone on board had been prepared for the transition: in the case of the humans it had meant the gagging-down of a pill big enough to choke a horse. But even that did not adequately minimize the effects of travelling through Dislocated space. I felt a terrible pressure at the back of my head and every right angle around me seemed to bend. I looked out of the porthole and saw the usual black of hyperspace turn to purple, permeated by flashes of red and blue that pulsed so rapidly that they seemed to burn holes in my brain. Then the pill took effect and reality returned. I shook myself mentally and got on with my work;

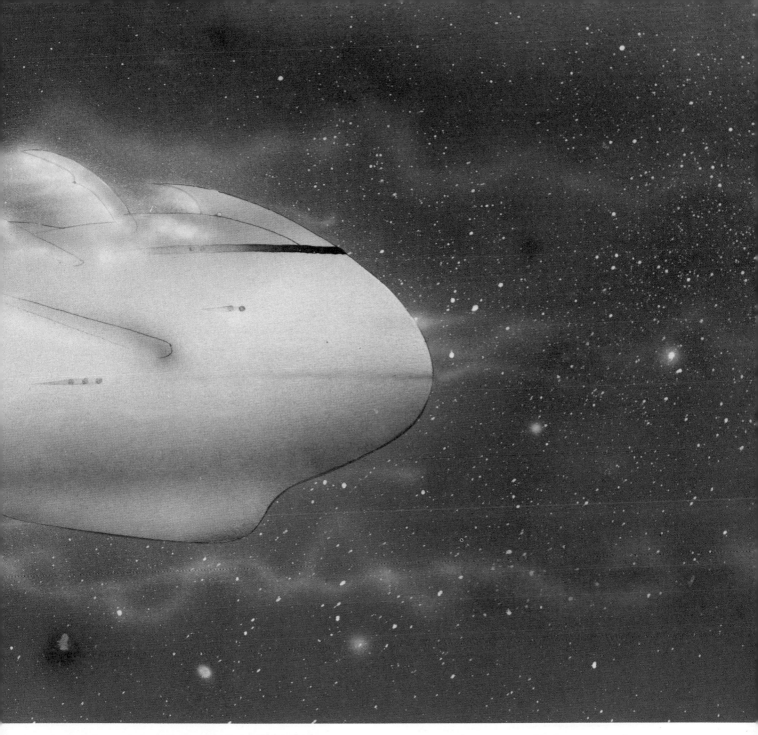

but after that experience I seldom looked out of the portholes when the Dislocation Drive was in operation. What was displayed outside was insidious enough to drive a human into madness. And subsequently I noticed that while the Drive was on the majority of the *Auriga's* portholes were covered: one design fault had become apparent.

The next few weeks were uneventful. Most of the scientists were happy: they scurried around, measuring the effects of the Drive on the ship's complement and equipment, had vast arguments about what they would find in N201 and prepared for the next major event. When the ship had traversed a quarter of the estimated distance it would drop out of hyperspace and, for the first time, it would be possible to view the home galaxy *in toto* with the naked eye. The soldiers, however, were extremely bored. There was nothing for them to do apart from the interminable drills and servicing of the *Auriga's* weaponry, and I had my work cut out to keep them supplied with liquor when they were off-duty. Have you ever tried to fill a bar order for 15 birds, 7 humanoids, 12 squid and 4½ leafy plants?

The moment arrived when the *Auriga* was to shift back into normal space. The scientists were almost hysterical with anticipation: but the military were hyper-tense: there was no telling what might happen when the ship re-emerged in unknown territory, and every soldier was at action-stations. The pressure and nausea reappeared as the ship dropped out of hyperspace. Force-shields went up around the ship and every parsec of space in the vicinity was examined for signs of hostile life. Only when the military and crew were completely satisfied were the scientists let loose. I took the opportunity to go out onto one of the viewing platforms.

In front of me was an achingly beautiful sight. Stretching right across the sky was a swirl of stars, so dense it looked like a slowly-rotating cloud. And every colour in the spectrum was represented, in combinations and permutations which reminded me of the most luscious music ever written. The Home Galaxy: and if anything was likely to convince me that there was a God it was the sheer grandeur of the spectacle. I looked around to see everyone else on the platform similarly transfixed: the *Auriga* had never been so silent. I turned to look in the opposite direction, towards N201, and made out a shining mist of stars, too far away to discern form, but close enough to suggest strangeness and a hint of menace.

We stayed where we were for a hundred ship-hours. I went null-gravity flying with other members of the crew and snoozed in the most comfortable bed in Creation, once you get used to it: empty, airless, gravityless space, with the stars as my mattress.

The scientists were finally satisfied and we set off again. Now the Dislocation Drive came into its own. Hitherto only cautious use had been made of it because of its experimental status, but from this point onwards the immense power of the Drive was unleashed and the ship sped through hyperspace at almost inconceivable speed. The scientists hastily revised their estimates of how long the trip would take: the projected time shrank from two years to six months. Almost too quick. . . yet, if it was possible to look at a ship travelling through hyperspace it would be a ghost, an insubstantial wraith, drifting at a snail's pace through a purple sea flecked with red and blue. The shape of the ship would change and twist and pour away in random directions, and time would seem to be standing still. . .

A month out from N201 the instruments began to pick up signals. The distortive effect of hyperspace made it impossible to identify them, so the captain decided to shift back into real space. So, just over 250,000 light-years out from N201, the *Auriga* dropped out of hyperspace and the computer and scientists got to work. It was rapidly established that the signals were not a natural phenomenon, but were being broadcast over a wide spectrum by a technologically-advanced species. This came as no surprise to the scientists: they had expected to find intelligence anyway, but closer analysis of the signals dumbfounded them. The message — if it *was* one — was being broadcast across the Deeps with a strength and clarity that was beyond the scope of current technology, and argued a very advanced civilization indeed. The scientists were arguing furiously amongst themselves when alarms sounded all over the ship. An intruder had entered our space.

The military were galvanized into activity. They took over control of the *Auriga* and placed all personnel on red alert. I was taken off normal duties and seconded to the bridge to assist in liaison. That's where I was when the first video pictures of the intruder came through. It was a spaceship of a completely unknown type, with a black, rakish body and,

stretching out behind it in every direction, something that looked suspiciously like a vast spider's web. It was coming from the direction of N201 at a tremendous speed. The scientists muttered incredulously as they watched the ship approach, for something strange was happening to the stars interposed behind the enormous web. They flickered and changed colour, and seemed to flow like heavy liquid as the intruder came closer. The scientists around me conjectured that the web was setting up a force-field of staggering dimensions and that this was being used to propel the ship. . . but *how?* Then the intruder stopped — dead. This caused even more alarm, for it was considered impossible for a spaceship to halt so quickly while under power in space. The *Auriga's* protective shields were already in operation and, for what seemed like an eon, the two ships examined each other. Then two blinding flashes of light stabbed out and the *Auriga* lurched. We were under attack.

Our protective shields absorbed most of the impact, but the rising whine of the engines

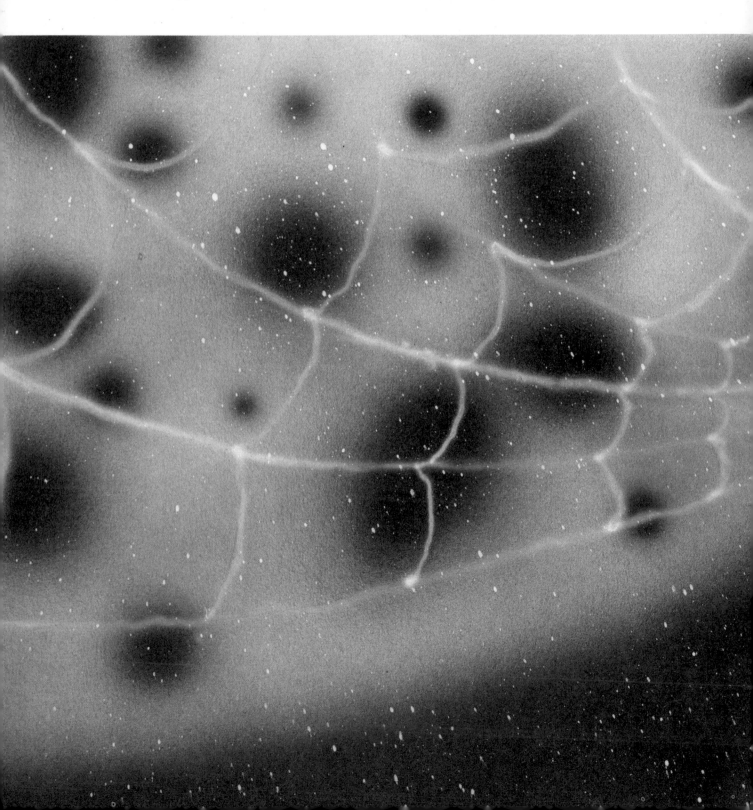

testified to the energy that had been drained by this first attack. The *Auriga* would not be able to take too much punishment of this nature. The military commander — an Andromedan — screamed in fury at the suddenness of the attack and ordered instant retaliation. A salvo of missiles flashed away from the *Auriga* towards a temptingly large target. . . But before they had travelled more than halfway there was a soundless explosion and they disappeared. The alien spaceship had obviously found a way of detonating the missiles while

they were in mid-flight. The commander swore and ordered the computer to fire more missiles in a random pattern, hoping that one, at least, might get through; he also let his men loose with laser cannon. Meanwhile, the alien had commenced firing continuously, and I knew enough about force-shields to imagine with horrible certainty what was happening to ours: as they absorbed more and more of the colossal energies being hurled in our direction they began to glow an angry red; sooner or later one of two things would happen — either they

would become completely saturated and would collapse, crushing the *Auriga,* or the power units that kept them in operation would overload and burn out. In either case we would be at the alien spaceship's mercy. Some of our missiles and laser fire, on the other hand, were getting through, but the alien seemed to have more effective shields than ours: they absorbed the impact with little more than a quiver. In less time than it takes to tell this the engagement was broken off. Our military commander, overwhelmingly aware of the enemy's superiority, ordered the *Auriga* to shift into hyperspace. We

this time we would not be able to escape. Travelling back across the Deeps was out of the question without the Dislocation Drive. And, at a conservative estimate, it would take roughly 2000 years for a message of help to get back to the home galaxy. And the alien spaceship had shown how advanced it was: it would probably be able to trace the course of the message laser, intercept it, and once it knew where the home galaxy was situated, attack without warning. The captain of the *Auriga* and the military commander finally came to a compromise. The ship had already travelled a long way from the

had been routed and our only hope was to escape in the limbo of hyperspace.

The alien spaceship did not — or could not — follow us. But the *Auriga* had been mortally wounded. A glum engineer listed the damage done. The shields would have to be repaired. The hull of the ship had been breached in two places — they had been sealed off, but many lives had been lost. Worst of all, the Dislocation Drive had been damaged. It would have to be fixed in real space. Even then he couldn't guarantee that repairs *were* possible.

This was disastrous. Returning to real space would leave us wide open to another attack, and

area where the battle had been fought. We could not be detected in hyperspace; there was a good chance that, if we continued retreating for about a week of ship-time, when we reappeared in real space the alien ship would have lost track of us. And if the worst happened and the ship was attacked again the star maps — which were the only indicators of where we had come from — would be destroyed.

A week later we dropped back into normal space. There was no sign of our attackers, and repairs were hurriedly commenced. The force-shields were reinforced before anything else was done, just in case; then work started on the

Drive. Every available person was put to work, but it seemed to be going very slowly: dismantling the shell of the drive took forever, and that was only the beginning.

As it happened, our frenetic activity was in vain. The alarms sounded again and all personnel once more took shelter inside the ship. The video screens confirmed the worst: the black ship was back. The *Auriga* was in a hopeless position. The repairs being attempted meant that the ship could not even hide in hyperspace. Our only hope was to make a stand. Gloriously romantic though the concept

I was in a vast, white-walled room, together with every member of the *Auriga* who had survived the final attack. Moving was difficult: it was as if I was swathed in cotton-wool, and I couldn't speak. There was no visible barrier around the small group that we constituted, but when I attempted to break out of the circle in which we were standing, I came up against an unyielding force-field. It was clear that we were prisoners.

At the other end of the room a green sphere materialized. Shadows formed inside and integrated into figures: hideous, sepia-scaled

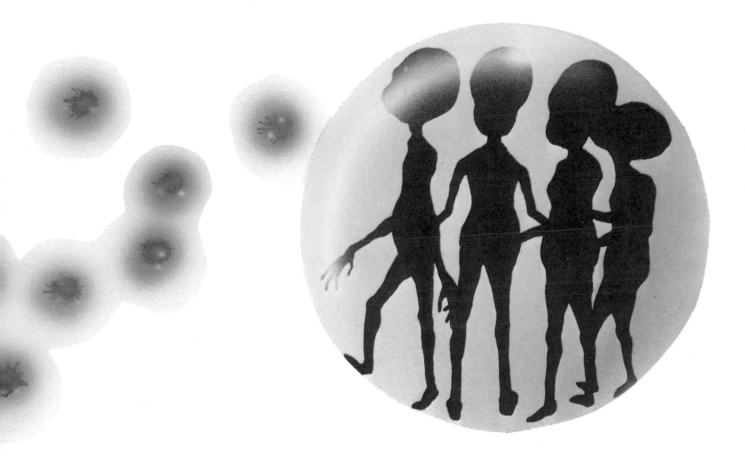

was, I had no illusions about what it meant. First the shields would collapse. Then the shell of the ship would be disintegrated by enemy fire. Everyone who had failed to get into a spacesuit would die a terrible death when his body exploded. The rest would be rounded up or eliminated at our attackers' leisure. . . The commander of the *Auriga*, with a hopeless expression of his face, gave the order for the star maps to be destroyed. All firing by our personnel ceased. The alien ship seemed to be measuring us for the final salvo, and I watched in total helplessness as two deadly shafts of light jabbed out.

creatures, about three metres tall, with enormous, unlidded, unblinking eyes: the stuff of which nightmares are made. They stirred and moving very slowly, tried to break out of the dome, but failed: they appeared to be prisoners just as we were. The tableau was frozen: we looked across at each other, in blank puzzlement.

Suddenly a dozen dancing blue balls appeared in the middle of the room. They darted around in the air at speed too quick for the eye to follow, from one side to the other, they regrouped in the centre of the room. They hung motionless in mid-air for a short time, then —

I felt a tickling inside my brain. It became persistent and painful, then dissolved and I heard a bell-like voice speaking inside my head.

"This is the Star Court. We are the Durg. We are the officers of this court. We police the Universe. We watched as you ventured across the Deeps. We watched as the Vrog attacked you. We ended the engagement before it got out of hand. We will now sit in judgement. The Vrog are the Defendants. They are across the room."

So those were the aliens who had attacked us! But, in that case, why were we imprisoned too? What was happening?

"The Vrog who attacked you will be punished. They have a lot to answer for. But they feared expansion into their galaxy. Rightly so. Rightly so. Your minds are open to us. We know your history well. Every species you represent has waged war in order to claim territory. Every time the destruction has been insane. Nothing in your minds convinces us that the pattern will change. You are a primitive galaxy, not ready to take up your appointed place in the Universe. You will be placed in quarantine. You will return to your own galaxy and stay there. We will decide when you may emerge. And your every action will be taken

into account before we remove the quarantine. That is the judgement of this court."

The blue balls disappeared. Nothing happened for a few minutes, then the dome enclosing the Vrog began to contract slowly. Agony appeared on their faces as the pressure mounted, and their mouths opened in silent screams. . .

I was back on board the *Auriga*. One look out of the porthole confirmed that the ship was in hyperspace and that the Drive had been repaired. The controls of the *Auriga* weren't responding, and the ship plunged implacably back to the home galaxy, out of our control.

As we approached home the ship dropped out of hyperspace. We could see our galaxy: it was as beautiful as ever, but there seemed to be a green nimbus around it, like that which imprisoned the Vrog. . .

Dr Caldwaller would have been delighted. The game finished before it really started.

The Race

My suit radio gave a preliminary whistle. I stopped work and switched to 'receive', glad of the break. It was Cort, the Aldebranian, and there was just a hint of agitation in his normally flat voice.

"Aren't the relays adjusted *yet,* Ben?"

"Just about. Only a couple of circuits to clear."

"Hurry, please. The race begins in five minutes. Out."

Five minutes! I cleared the last two circuits in one, was in the airlock, pulling off my suit in two and was sitting in the viewing-room in three. Cort was already there, as was every other member of the space-station; the room was humming with conversations in a dozen languages. I was flanked by a couple of Andromedans, who were arguing furiously, beaks snapping and wings flapping, about the merits of one competitor over another. I tuned them out, yelled to Cort that the relays were integrated and the Aldebranian switched on.

The viewing-screen exploded with colour. Then the picture steadied, and the conversations died out. The image was wonderfully clear: even the tenuous, web-like sails of the ships staggered around the beacon could be seen. The scene was quite lovely — three hundred graceful craft, sparkling like jewels, poised motionless against the backdrop of deep purple interstellar space studded with stars; in one corner of the picture a double sun, two red giants which seemed to be reaching out to devour each other, balanced by the majestic green bulge of the planet Etta in the foreground. The voice of the commentator impinged, droning out the odds on each ship. It seemed that the Stygian vessel, the *Orion,* was currently favourite to win; my own choice, on which I had bet 100 intergalactic credits, was way down in the rankings.

This was the biggest event of the racing season. Shortly the three hundred ships, powered only by solar sails, would set off from

Etta, in the Krell system, and would streak through space to Riga, the finishing-point for the race. A distance of 100 light-years, and every metre would be hotly contested. The entire Galaxy would come to a halt for a full Standard Day while the race was run. This was unquestionably the most popular spectator sport ever devised and virtually every sentient being in the Galaxy would be riveted to the viewscreen until the winner of the race was declared.

The commentator's voice cracked hysterically as the beacon flashed, signifying the start of the race. An instant, which felt like an eternity, as the sails of the ships swung around to catch the merest whisper of the solar wind; then one ship, the black, pencil-thin Jakon *Fordax* broke away from the cluster around the beacon and launched itself in the direction of the double sun. It was followed immediately by a group of six ships, which included the *Orion* and my own selection, the *Pertwhistle,* the only entry from the Solar System. The rest of the field streamed out behind this leading group, and the race was on.

Pandemonium reigned in the viewing room. Every creature, including myself, was standing, screaming at the screen — imprecations, cajolings, joy and despair; from the corner of my eye I could see two willowy plants dancing a stately jig with each other. They had obviously backed the leader, and the first ship away from the pack had an enormous advantage. The Andromedans next to me muttered sourly.

One of the main reasons for the popularity of solar wind racing as a spectator sport was the element of danger. Of the three hundred ships which started, only a couple of dozen would reach the finishing-point. Not being able to travel through hyperspace, each craft was subject to the usual hazards of normal space — everything ranging from gravitational fields to comets — along with two additional perils: the vagaries of the solar winds and the whims of the organisers. The race resembled an obstacle course of a particularly deadly kind. The ships were routed through areas of space which no-one in full sanity would enter. This course involved travelling *between* the two suns mentioned earlier, going into an area infested by minute anti-matter debris and even skirting the edge of a black hole. Television cameras were positioned strategically along the route to bring us pictures of every catastrophe; it was even possible to watch the crews of each ship at work — or their dying agonies. And we drank in every minute of it.

The hubbub in the room settled down to a murmur as we watched the string of ships approach the first hazard — the double sun. Then we were watching the crew of the *Fordax* at work as they jockeyed the ship into position to effect entry, and the camera zoomed in to focus on the face of the captain, who looked a bit like a fish with blue and pink wattles — and scared . . . then we were in space again, observing the

ship as it was buffeted by the colossal energies poured out by the two suns, and I could almost feel the heat searing my face; the cameras veered away and focussed on the second ship as it entered the strait. The rising murmur in the room attested to the fact that the captain had chosen the wrong line, and we watched in complete fascination as the craft, the *Brique*, seemed to stagger and was drawn implacably towards the furnace of one of the suns. Then it had disappeared, and we were back on board

double sun had been a matter of skill, here luck was the only factor which played a part. Meanwhile, the competitors were flashing through space and the commentators were listing the craft which had been lost, to a chorus of groans from the assembled company . . . altogether 18 ships had disappeared into one or the other of the suns, but *Pertwhistle* had made it. That was encouraging.

Now we discovered why the *Orion* had been made the favourite. Every ship was under full

the *Fordax* as it emerged into clear space. There was a spontaneous burst of applause in the room and one of the Andromedans remarked that it looked like being a wonderful race.

There was now a relatively easy run to the next hazard, the remnants of a planetary system which had been shattered by some cataclysm a very long time ago. All that was left of the system were microscopic particles of anti-matter, just one of which was enough to destroy a ship totally. And, whereas negotiating the

power now, and the solar wind was being milked for all the energy it could provide; in terms of real space phenomenal speeds were being attained. Yet the *Orion* drifted past the two ships in front of it with contemptuous ease and was within shouting distance of the *Fordax* when it plunged into the devastated system.

There can be nothing more frightening in the Universe than drifting through the blackness of this area of space, knowing that you are surrounded by particles which are extremely difficult to detect and which could obliterate you in an instant. The ultimate variation of that ancient game known as Russian Roulette. Prudently, video equipment had not been installed inside this area and we were confined to looking at a grid on which the position of each ship within the system was indicated, alternated with long shots in which the ships looked like insects marching across a black canvas, and close-ups of the crews. We watched spellbound as the ships inched through this system. Occasionally one of them would flare

Pertwhistle was third and a new ship, the *Tyx*, was moving up fast. We all relaxed marginally: I felt drained by the tension of the previous stage. Other members of the station moved around the room, stretching limbs and snatching bites to eat; no-one, however, strayed too far from the view screen, which showed the leading ships keeping formation. The final hazard was coming up shortly, and it would be the most spectacular and dangerous of all. This involved skipping off the edge of a black hole —

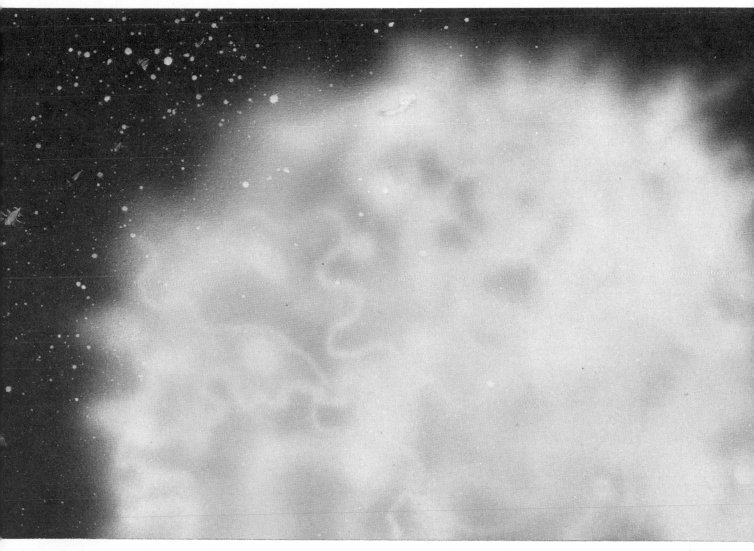

up, throwing out a light that was so bright that my eyes shut in pain and the afterimage was burnt onto my retinas for some time after. And running over and through my concentration was the voice of the commentator, tallying up the ships lost: before this system was traversed 80 ships had been destroyed and we had witnessed the death agonies of the crews for at least half that number.

The race finally moved into clear space again. At some stage *Orion* had passed *Fordax* and had opened up a substantial lead;

a manoeuvre which, if properly executed, could treble the velocity of the ship. But the tiniest miscalculation and the ship would be drawn into the hole and would collapse into itself like a dying sun. It was no wonder that the air of relaxation in the room in which I was sitting seemed to extend to the ships taking part in the race: it was a time for recovery, of preparing for the ultimate trial.

I grabbed a sandwich and was back in my place when the viewscreen showed the *Orion* approaching the black hole. The room was totally silent now: in previous races this sort of hazard had accounted for ninety per cent of the competitors left at this stage.

The black hole was exactly that: the only indication that it was there was a circle of stars which were completely blacked out. The *Orion*, followed by the *Fordax* and the *Pertwhistle*, seemed to scuttle sideways to the edge of the hole. When the ship made the most tenuous of contacts the results were spectacular. The *Orion* was bathed in a firework display of cosmic proportions. It disappeared for a few seconds in the maelstrom of colour and when it was visible again it looked like a comet with a tail of blue fire. And its speed had increased quite perceptibly . . . the camera cut to the interior of the ship: there was exultation in the faces of the crew as they rode the whirlwind all the way to possible victory. The *Fordax* wasn't so lucky. The captain chose a slightly different angle at which to glance off the black hole and the miscalculation was disastrous. No fireworks this time: the *Fordax* stopped dead. Inexorably, like a fisherman reeling in, the black hole sucked the *Fordax* into its heart. The ship crumpled up into a tiny ball of silver foil and was gone. The *Pertwhistle* shared the same fate, to my intense chagrin, as did seventy other ships, according to the commentator; it looked very much as if the *Orion* was home and dry and that the race was, to all intents and purposes, over. Or was it?

The *Tyx*, more through good luck than the skill of the crew, made a perfect contact with the edge of the black hole. Pyrotechnics, and the ship had cut the *Orion*'s lead to a minimum. Riga was only a short distance away now, and our excitement had us screaming at the viewscreen, willing the *Tyx* on. And the *Tyx*, an outsider at 50-1 before the race started, was drawing closer and closer, thanks to the impetus it had gained from the black hole. Two parsecs away from Riga it passed the *Orion* and a few seconds later it was streaking through the laser beam which stretched from Riga to one of its moons — the finishing line — and a highly popular winner.

The room exploded. For a long while the voice of the commentator was drowned out by the noise. When the level of celebration had finally dropped I staggered back to my seat to watch the presentation ceremonies. While we waited for the crew of the *Tyx* to be ferried down to Riga where nearly a million sentient beings were waiting to greet them, the

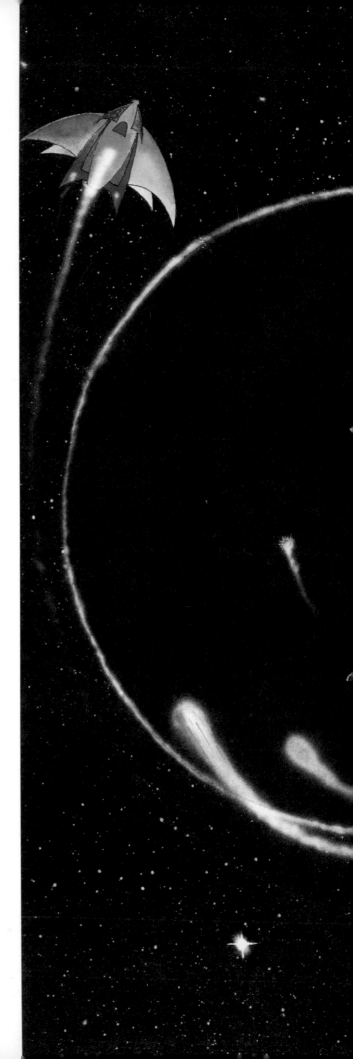

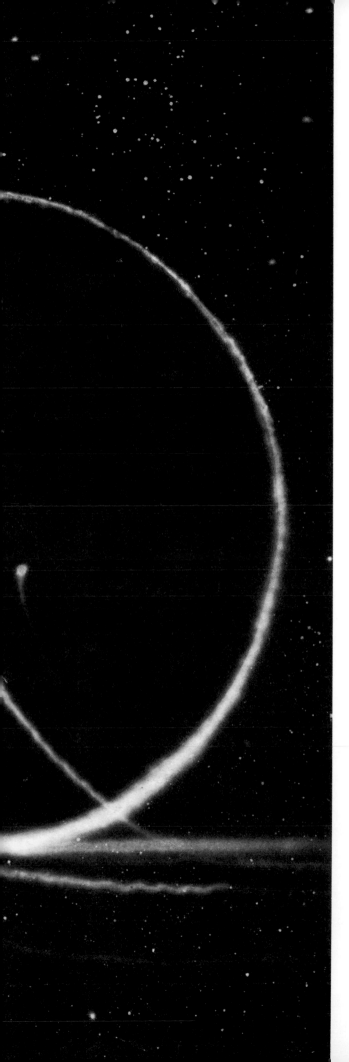

commentator listed the ships which had failed to finish: 195 in all, lower than in the previous race, but still well over half that had set off from Etta.

The crews of the *Tyx* and *Orion* arrived, and were presented with first and second prizes: 5,000,000 and 2,000,000 credits respectively. Every other competitor in the race was applauded and received a smaller sum on arrival. Then there was a slight hiatus and the crowd stirred restlessly; finally, to overwhelming cheers, the crews of the ships which had been *destroyed* appeared. A new set of presentations were made, for the most spectacular destruction, the best acting and the best turned-out crew.

Didn't you know? The race is a simulation from beginning to end. The crews are all actors, the ships are props. The Central Computer designs the race, and no-one, except for the actors themselves and the organisers, all sworn to secrecy, know how it will come out. It is still a race and a spectacle for the uncountable billions who watch — but did you really believe that the Galactic Federation would allow ships and lives to be lost this way?

We're *civilised* now, you know.

Time Travel

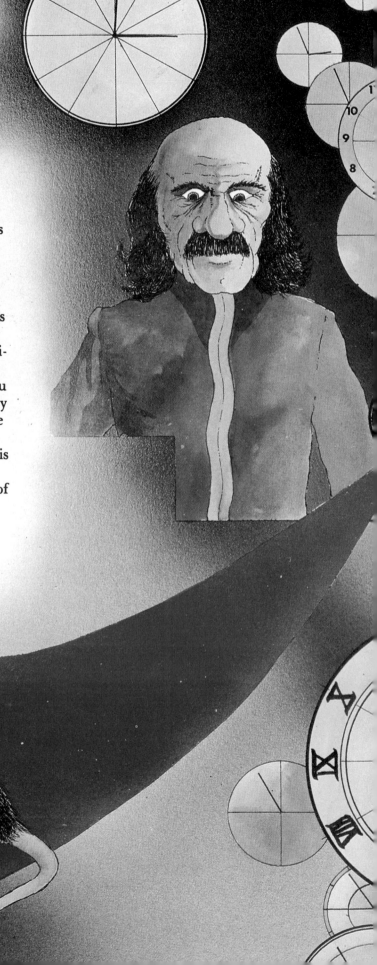

Llorrac Siwel, the doyen of all the inter-galactic video commentators, is broadcasting from the laboratory of the most prominent scientist in the Universe, Professor 'Duke' Millington. This is one of the scientific occasions of the millenium. The professor has perfected his theory of time travel and is about to put it to the test.

Siwel is commentating for the benefit of every sentient being in the known Universe. His voice is hushed; his audience hangs on his every word.

"The professor is now making the final cali-brations. I wish you were all here to witness this historic event with me, and I am sure you all share my absolute admiration for this truly great man. Now he is standing back from the machine. He appears to have finished all his preparations. The tension is unbearable. He is looking over the room packed with eminent scientists, and he is smiling: he is convinced of the accuracy of his theory. Now! He has placed the cage containing the rat in the middle of the field. This rat will be the first creature in Creation to travel backwards in time. And the professor presses the button . . . ."

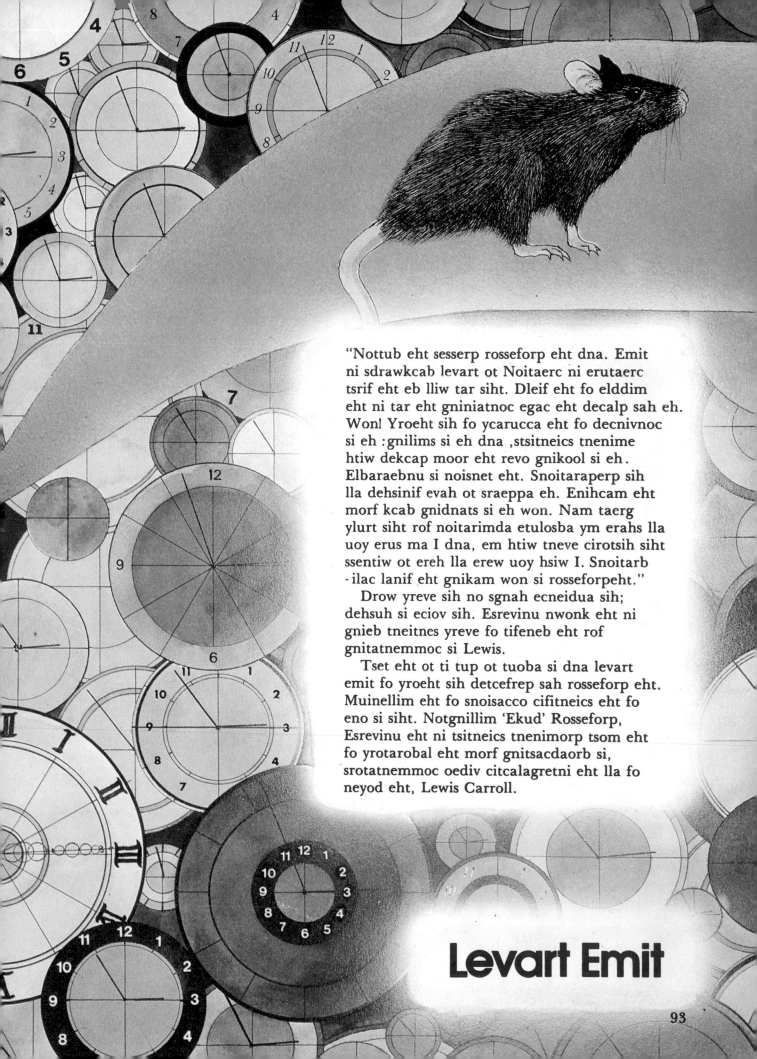

"Nottub eht sesserp rosseforp eht dna. Emit ni sdrawkcab levart ot Noitaerc ni erutaerc tsrif eht eb lliw tar siht. Dleif eht fo elddim eht ni tar eht gniniatnoc egac eht decalp sah eh. Won! Yroeht sih fo ycarucca eht fo decnivnoc si eh :gnilims si eh dna ,stsitneics tnenime htiw dekcap moor eht revo gnikool si eh. Elbaraebnu si noisnet eht. Snoitaraperp sih lla dehsinif evah ot sraeppa eh. Enihcam eht morf kcab gnidnats si eh won. Nam taerg ylurt siht rof noitarimda etulosba ym erahs lla uoy erus ma I dna, em htiw tneve cirotsih siht ssentiw ot ereh lla erew uoy hsiw I. Snoitarb- ilac lanif eht gnikam won si rosseforpeht."

Drow yreve sih no sgnah ecneidua sih; dehsuh si eciov sih. Esrevinu nwonk eht ni gnieb tneitnes yreve fo tifeneb eht rof gnitatnemmoc si Lewis.

Tset eht ot ti tup ot tuoba si dna levart emit fo yroeht sih detcefrep sah rosseforp eht. Muinellim eht fo snoisacco cifitneics eht fo eno si siht. Notgnillim 'Ekud' Rosseforp, Esrevinu eht ni tsitneics tnenimorp tsom eht fo yrotarobal eht morf gnitsacdaorb si, srotatnemmoc oediv citcalagretni eht lla fo neyod eht, Lewis Carroll.

Levart Emit